Books by Norma Johnston

The Keeping Days
Glory in the Flower
The Sanctuary Tree
A Mustard Seed of Magic
Strangers Dark and Gold
Of Time and Of Seasons
A Striving After Wind
The Swallow's Song
If You Love Me, Let Me Go
The Crucible Year
Pride of Lions
A Nice Girl Like You
Myself and I
The Days of the Dragon's Seed
Timewarp Summer
Gabriel's Girl

GABRIEL'S

GIRL

GABRIEL'S

GIRL

by Norma Johnston

ATHENEUM   New York   1983

LIBRARY OF CONGRESS CATALOGING IN PUBLICATION DATA

Johnston, Norma.
Gabriel's girl.

SUMMARY: *Sarah finds she has embarked on a dangerous*
mission in Spain when she searches for her father,
a famous exposé writer, who has mysteriously
disappeared from his hotel.
[1. Mystery and detective stories.   2. Fathers
and daughters—Fiction.   3. Spain—Fiction]
I. Title.
PZ7.J6453Gal   1983   [Fic]   83-2631
ISBN 0-689-30989-9

Published simultaneously in Canada by
McClelland & Stewart, Ltd.
Composition by Service Typesetters, Austin, Texas
Printed and bound
by Fairfield Graphics, Fairfield, Pennsylvania
Designed by Mary Ahern
First Edition

*For two Junes—
one English,
one American*

GABRIEL'S

GIRL

1

My name is Sarah Gabriel Langham. My father is Gabriel Langham, the author of all those "what really happened behind the headlines" exposé books, and all my life I've been known as "Gabriel's girl." Part of me likes that. I'm proud of him and of the closeness that's the inevitable result, I suppose, of Mother having died when I was young. But another part of me, by the time I was sixteen, wanted to scream every time I heard it: "Look at me! I am Sarah! I'm a person, too, not just Gabe Langham's daughter." I didn't, of course. I didn't even tell Dad, which was really crazy, for he of all people would have understood.

But this isn't the story of what it's like to be a celebrity's daughter. Instead, it's the story of what happened to me when I was seventeen and my world turned upside down.

"Begin where the action starts." How often I've heard Dad hand out that advice, looking at me over the top of his glasses as I struggled with a school assignment. The action this time started with a telephone call on an afternoon in May, when I'd just come home from school.

No, not from school. I'd just come from the hospital where Selena, our housekeeper for years, was nursing indignation and a broken leg. Selena'd slipped on a wet patch in the laundry room, and now she'd been ordered to recuperate for a month at her married daughter's, where there were no stairs to climb. I calmed Selena down and tried to convince her (a) the doctor was not insulting her, (b) the doctor was not implying she was too old to work, (c) I was a big girl now and could look after myself till she was back in fighting trim. Then I went home to persuade my father over the telephone of that same last point.

Critics have said that what makes Dad's non-fiction books so successful is his ability to capture the whole mood of an experience in a few sharp details. I can understand that now. I can remember how warm and bright the sunlight was, making parallellograms on the polished floor. I can remember the branch of dogwood in the blue vase on the hall table. I remember thinking Dad had brought that vase from Japan, and wondering what he would bring me from this trip to Spain. I remember checking the mailbox to see if there was another letter, knowing it was unlikely because one had come just the day before. I remember flicking through the mail quickly, watching for a foreign stamp, then tossing it aside with my schoolbooks. And digging out yesterday's letter, flattening it, trying to decipher Dad's tiny, cryptic writing. Wishing, not for the first time, that the great author would break down and write his letters on the battered portable he lugged with him around the world. But no, Dad liked to scribble lines to me whenever the spirit moved him—in police courts, pubs, bistros, planes—and he scribbled them on anything that he found handy. I have one whole set of letters from southern Europe written on what he called "a representative selection of the latest issues, *genus* toilet paper." *This* letter was on proper air mail stationery, pale blue, printed with his newest address.

Apartemento la Colomba
Torremolinos, España

Dad had taken off last week for the south of Spain, but I didn't know why. He never tells me the exact nature of the trail he's on when he first starts researching a new book. "That way none of my dear friends and deadly competitors can wheedle it out of you," he says, winking. I sometimes think his caution is more likely the result of his years in the diplomatic service. Anyway, once his book thesis "jells," as he puts it, he always tells me and only me, outside of his agent. That is another mark of trust that makes me "Gabriel's girl." Only this time, right from the start, things were—different. One night Dad had a couple of mysterious after-midnight phone calls. The next morning, to my astonishment, I found him packing his bags.

"I have to go to Torremolinos, right away. And don't bother asking if you can come. You have your gymnastics competition next week, remember? Not to mention those two exams." I kicked myself for having let him know about them, and Dad saw my look and grinned. "Cheer up. It will be summer soon, and I'll take you with me then, no matter what."

"Where?" I demanded uncompromisingly, and Dad shrugged.

"Don't know yet. England to jump off from, probably. Then maybe Ireland. Germany. Or Italy."

I remember thinking he was avoiding the issue with that string of unrelated places. And once more he saw and read my look, and his eyes twinkled. That's one of the special things we have, Dad and I; the ability to almost read each other's minds.

"You wouldn't have much fun this trip anyway," Dad said. "I don't know how long I'll be gone or where I'll end up." He fished a piece of paper from his pocket. "I do have a starting address though. I just phoned that rental condominium outfit that's been advertising so much on the radio. At the price, the places sound too good to be true: all furnished, everything from sauna to supermarket on the premises. But at least it will be a place to park my bags and Bozo." Bozo is the aforementioned battered typewriter. "I'll write as soon as I check in, and send my room number, and then you can phone me once a week like we always do."

So he'd written, as he'd promised. "In haste, in the lobby, waiting for desk clerk. It's siesta time. I was right, those ads were too good to be true. It'll do, though. Don't phone—you could have trouble reaching me. *I'll* call *you*, Sunday, usual time. Guess what? Uncle Tom's at hdqtrs. in Madrid. Nice seeing him again. Trail looks promising—wish me luck."

He'd signed his letter the way he always did to me: *Bad Penny*. "Because, like a bad penny, you can always count on me to turn up," he'd told me long ago. *I* suspected the phrase could be one more example of his mania for secrecy. My friend Callie is convinced that Bad Penny is Dad's undercover code name. Callie's absolutely sure that scandal-sheet story last year "exposing" Dad as a CIA agent is gospel truth, and Dad's telling her it was a pack of lies did no good at all.

Beneath the signature, as usual, Dad had scribbled his room number—1327. I remember thinking that hotels and offices in the States usually don't have a thirteenth floor because it's thought bad luck.

"Uncle Tom" was Tom McLean, my godfather and Dad's oldest friend, and "hdqtrs." meant the U. S. Embassy. I remember chuckling about Dad's automatic ambiguousness as I picked up the phone and punched the direct-dial numbers. Today was Tuesday, and if I waited till Sunday night to tell him about Selena's accident, Dad would be sore. Besides, Callie was urging me to move into her house for the duration of his trip.

The telephone gave out strange tunes and odd, foreign ringings. It rang and rang for a long, long time. What time was it in Spain now? Long past siesta time, I was to remember thinking. But that was later, when I'd had grim personal experience with that hotel switchboard. Right now it was 4:15 p.m. in our New Jersey suburb, and I was tapping my fingers impatiently, knowing Callie might burst in at any moment.

At last, far away and foggy, a man's voice. "La Colomba."

"Mr. Gabriel Langham, please. Room 1327."

"*Non parla Inglese.*"

Rats, I thought, and searched frantically for the words Callie used to singsong aloud as she struggled with

Spanish I. "*Cuarto trece veinte siete. Señor* Langham."

"*No está aqui.*"

"I *know* he's not there. I want you to get—" I started automatically in English as the expensive transatlantic minutes mounted. Would he understand any French? "*Voulez-vous—*"

The line went dead.

The front door banged open, and Callie's head popped inside. "Sarah are you coming? I've got Mom's car. If we hurry we can get over to Fairview Regional and case the competition before their practice lets out." Fairview was our arch rival in that state gymnastics competition.

"I can't yet. I'm trying to reach my father." I frowned, punching the phone buttons again with concentration. "We got cut off; I don't know what happened. All I could make out was a man saying Senor Langham *no está aqui.*"

"Maybe he never got there! Or maybe he's underground." Callie, big-eyed, was hoping for the worst as usual.

"Don't be ridiculous," I said tartly, and thrust the phone at her. "Here. *You* try this time. You owe me something for helping you memorize vocabulary lists the past three years."

Callie gave me a look, cleared her throat, and assumed her most imperious Spanish señorita voice.

The result was the same. Señor Langham could not be called. Señor Langham was not there.

I looked at Callie, and Callie said helpfully, "Maybe you got the wrong hotel."

"No, I didn't. Dad told me the name before he left,

and here it is on the stationery, with that phone number."

"Maybe that was a red herring." Callie was clinging to her CIA delusion. "To throw people off while he went underground."

"Don't be melodramatic," I said automatically. But I was growing increasingly uneasy, remembering the ways in which *this* trip of Dad's was different from all the others. That was the worst thing about Callie's fantasies: however farfetched, they always had one grain of possibility that made me shaky. Callie, whose heart is as big as her imagination, said quickly, "Isn't there anybody else who might know where to reach him?"

"His editor," I said gratefully, and punched the number.

The editor was out on a business trip. His secretary didn't know how he could be reached.

His agent was in her office with a client. After a tussle with the switchboard dragon, I was put through.

"Sarah, how nice to hear from you," Monica McCausland said warmly. "Have you news for me from your father?"

"I was hoping *you* might, for me. I just called his hotel, and they acted as if they'd never heard of him. Do you know where he could be?"

Miss McCausland must have caught my anxiety, for her voice sobered. "I'm afraid not, Sarah. He called me from the airport to say he was on his way to Spain, but that was all."

"Can't you just this once tell me what Dad's working on? I know you can't say it now, with someone in your office—"

"It's not that, Sarah," Miss McCausland interrupted.

"I really don't know. This time Gabe wouldn't even tell me. He said he didn't have enough evidence yet, but this was something really big, something that would destroy a lot of sacred cows. So he didn't want to breathe a word until he had more proof. I gathered something had just happened to make him think he could get proof if he acted quickly."

There was a slight pause, as though she were thinking hard. "He said if he was right, it could be the most important book he's ever written, but it could kick up a dreadful ruckus. Then he laughed and said forget about the pen being mightier than the sword, he was going to prove the typewriter was mightier than the TV camera. I remember thinking he must have gotten his idea from something he'd seen recently on TV. Sarah, if it's really important for you to reach your father, you might try the London agency we're associated with. He said he might be in touch with them." She gave me the name, address and number, and rang off.

"What's the matter?" Callie asked, looking at my face. I told her, briefly. Her eyes grew large. "Oh, Sarah, you don't suppose he's been kidnapped do you?"

"Don't be ridiculous!"

"No, I'm serious. We keep forgetting that your dad's real famous. And there's all those secrets he's digging up, not to mention what he knows from the CIA. Somebody could think he's worth a lot of money." Callie has inflated ideas about our income, as well as about Dad's past. "No, now don't just shrug it off. There's been a lot of kidnappings of important people by terrorists, for ransom and stuff. Don't you remember last year—"

"You watch too much TV," I started to snap. The

words died in my throat. A memory flashed before my eyes, clear as an image on a TV screen. Dad and myself, last year, watching a news broadcast . . . an American military attaché had been held hostage. Tense waiting for the ransom demands . . . wild speculation about terrorist groups. Talk of the IRA, the PLO, the Red Brigade. . . .

And Dad shaking his head, saying, "It's not that simple." Saying, "They're on the wrong track, those groups must have more hot cash than they know what to do with." And then, in that half-to-himself tone I knew so well, "*I wonder . . .*"

If Dad was on the trail of terrorist group cash flow, he could indeed be onto something big. And he could indeed be in danger.

Monica McCausland had said she thought Dad's idea had come from something on TV.

In that TV report, there had been accounts of undercover agents who had asked too many questions—and had disappeared. Sometimes not even their bodies had been found. The thought terrified me. And from somewhere inside came a determination to do something.

Behind me, the grandfather's clock chimed five. Callie's voice, soft with concern, said, "It won't do any good to stand here worrying. Come on over to Fairview for the last few minutes. You can stay with us tonight and try to call your dad again."

"*No*," I said firmly, and snatched up my purse. "Drive me to the bank quick. I have to get my college money out of my savings account before the drive-in window closes. And then I'll have to call the airlines."

By ten that night, I was on a plane to Malaga.

2

The morning sun was hot, and the scent of Mediterranean flowers came through the taxi's open window. To my left, down the cliffs, the Mediterranean sparkled, sublimely blue. I breathed deeply, wishing my pulses would stop pounding. I felt lightheaded, and as though the bottom had dropped out of my stomach—and no wonder. It was not just night-flight jet lag. There had been the rush to Kennedy Airport, with Callie's father at the wheel. Before that, a frantic hour and a half locating my passport and locating the credit cards that Dad had issued to me "for emergencies." This *was* an emergency, something insisted in my brain. And somehow I had convinced Callie's family of that, too. I threw a few changes of clothes haphazardly into a small suitcase and a carry-on duffle bag, not sure what to pack or how long I would be gone. Dad's letter went in my shoulder bag, along with my college money.

I had taken the envelope out, to show the hotel address to the driver who could not understand my pronunciation.

Here it was now, a group of modern whitewashed towers against the brilliant sky, the name blazoned on the nearest roof. A jungle of tropical vegetation lined the drive.

The cabbie dumped my luggage on the terra-cotta entrance tiles and roared away.

The lobby was cool and spacious and still, and a fountain splashed among greenery at its center. On the far side, the long marble reception counter was deserted.

At last a young Spaniard in an impeccable business suit appeared and looked at me oddly. I flushed, conscious of my dishevelled state, wondering if wearing jeans to arrive in a Latin country had been wise. I drew myself up and assumed what Dad calls my "lady of the household tone."

"Do you speak English?" He nodded. "Mr. Gabriel Langham, please."

"Mr. Langham is not here."

"I'll wait." The room seemed to be going around— clearly I had not gotten enough sleep on the plane—and I clutched at the edge of the counter hastily. "Could I wait in his room, please? I'm his daughter."

I fished in my bag for my identifying passport. The manager didn't look at it. He didn't look in the guest registry, either. He merely said, "No Langham staying here," and turned away.

"But he must be! He's in Room 1327. Look!" I could hear my voice climbing perilously as I produced the now-crumpled letter. The manager could not have cared less. He said again, flatly, "No Langhams here," and gave me an exceedingly blank stare.

What the dickens was Spanish for thirteen-twenty-seven? I enunciated carefully. *"Cuarto trece veinte siete,* Will you please check your records?"

This time he did condescend to say, "No. Room thirteen-twenty-seven a Swedish family. Come for the summer." Clearly, to his mind, the subject was closed. The hell it was, I thought grimly. I had reached the swear-word stage, and I was suddenly too tired to push further now.

"Then I want a room for myself. Immediately. I do not know yet how long I will be staying." I flashed my credit card ostentatiously, in case there was any question of my ability to pay.

For a minute he hesitated, his gaze not blank any longer, but suspicious. Then he shrugged and pushed the registration pad forward. "Room not ready yet. Maids not finished."

"When will it be?" Another shrug. "Is there some-place where I can get lunch?"

He gestured in a way I took to mean *downstairs-outside-toward the beach.* "You go now. We bring bags up to room when ready." I hesitated, glancing at the bags, and he said again, firmly, "We take care. You go."

Apparently that was the way things were done here. And I needed to eat. And to do some hard thinking . . . although there was no use trying until my head was clear. I left suitcase and duffle and still wearing my shoulder purse made my way across the deserted lobby and out a side door to the path around the building.

How can I describe the sensations that arose? Maybe I wouldn't have felt them if I hadn't been so tired and worried, if the manager's manner hadn't made me sure that something was definitely wrong. As it was, I had the sensation of stepping into the reality behind a stage-set La Colomba presented to the world. The pink cement of the path was cracked. The vines and shrubs, lush with flowers, reached out to brush me, as though a garden once carefully tended had gone wild. Where there were steps, spiderwebs lurked in the railings. The ground sloped sharply toward the sea, so that what was basement level at La Colomba's front became the first floor in the back. There were stores there. Correction: there had been stores, or were going to be stores. Signs said *pelugueria, libreria, supermercado*, but the windows were boarded up or painted over. No wonder Dad had said those radio descriptions proved "too good to be true."

Where was he, anyway?

From behind a half-curtained doorway came the unmistakable smell of olive oil, rancid and smoking. Suddenly I had to get away. I left the buildings, hurrying down some steps, and found myself looking toward the sea across a sloping, empty, path-crossed lot. There was a road along the shore, with wide walks on either side, and there were cabanas on the beach. Where there were cabanas and bathhouses, there were food stands.

I walked swiftly down the twisting footpath, stumbling on stones, taking great gulps of the fresh sea air. A scrawny rooster with his chicken harem watched me curiously, and an equally scrawny goat thrust his nose at my handbag hopefully.

"Sorry, nothing this time. Maybe I'll bring you something later." I scratched his ears, and the tight knot inside of me started to ease. Surely, my anxiety was out of all proportion. If I just stayed here for a day or so, Dad would turn up, the proverbial bad penny.

Bad penny. A code name, Callie insisted. It was a crazy idea. Or was it? Dad never let his face be shown on TV, or on book jackets. It would make him too easy to identify when he was poking around anonymously, he insisted. For all I knew, he could have registered at La Colomba under another name. Maybe that was why he had written me not to telephone him. Being Dad, he would never have entrusted his pseudonym to a letter.

In which case, all I'd have to do was hang around La Colomba until I saw him. How he would laugh at my apprehensions!

Somehow I needed very much to hear that laughter.

I ate a kind of shish-kebab at a shorefront stand, and some flat Spanish bread, and drank strong coffee. It was black and bitter, but it put starch in my spine. I walked back to La Colomba feeling somewhat better, collected the key to my room, and went upstairs.

It was twelve thirty-nine. Twelve stories up. I had forgotten Europeans started counting from the first floor *above* the ground. By American reckoning, I was on the thirteenth floor.

It wasn't just a room, but a studio apartment. This was an *apartment* hotel. Tiled bath (with no towels); tiled kitchenette with small European-style stove and re-frigerator; small square room with plastic-covered mod-ern chair and sofa, a modern wall of built-ins, a hanging globe light over a table and chairs. Sliding glass doors opening onto a balcony, facing away from the sea into a cold north light.

It was everything a young career girl could wish for

in an apartment, but all the same I felt a chill.

My luggage wasn't there. I looked around for a phone to call the front desk and felt another chill. There was no phone. There had been. Black wires protruded from a hole in the wall; but the instrument was gone.

I would have to go downstairs. I opened the door, and there was my suitcase, sitting in the corridor a few yards away. I must have walked right past it when I came up, I thought. Or else it had arrived in the past few minutes. In which case why hadn't the bellboy brought it to the room? And where was my duffle? There was nothing here in the hall but my little suitcase.

A girl whisked out of a nearby room, younger than I, wearing a maid's uniform. She saw me and smiled, and when I motioned to her, she came. But when I tried to ask about my duffle, she shook her head.

"*Non habla Inglese.*"

"*Français?*"

"*Si—un peu.*" In our schoolroom French, we managed a kind of communication. But again she shook her head. She had not seen the missing duffle. I would have to go report it downstairs.

The manager who registered me was no longer at the desk. The new man spoke less English and regarded what I said as definitely fishy. Why had I left my bags at the desk? Because the manager had told me to, since my room was not ready. Then why was I not in my room, waiting for them, when the bellboy had been able to bring them up? Out of the building? Why had I not taken my suitcases with me? Bellboys were not allowed to enter guest bedrooms in guests' absence. My being out had necessitated their being left in the hall, where anyone could take them. Clearly, I was responsible. I should consider myself fortunate that *both* bags were not missing.

My request that he report the theft to the police was greeted by a torrent of protesting Spanish. At last the other desk manager appeared, and I turned to him in relief. To my disbelief, he shook his head.

"You do not want to go to the police. They will say it is your fault for leaving your bags out of your sight. They will wonder what was in those bags that was so valuable. They will wonder why you came here alone, with no reservation. A young girl in a foreign country does not want to get mixed up with the police."

His voice was matter-of-fact, but the implication was a threat. I felt my body starting to shake and willed it to behave. What would Dad do now, I wondered wildly, and dug in my heels. I had nothing to hide from the police. That duffle bag contained personal belongings that I wanted back. "No drugs, and no contraband," I finished flatly.

Was it my imagination or did I intercept a cryptic glance between the men? I wondered if, and how, I had struck a nerve. I was suddenly inspired to add, "If the police do not believe me, I can call my friend at our embassy in Madrid."

There was no mistaking the glance this time. The manager suddenly became suave. Of course, if I insisted, they would take me personally to the police—*mañana*. As a special favor to a hysterical female, his tone implied. But first they would instruct the maids to look for the missing duffle in other rooms. Perhaps it had been left in the wrong corridor. The bellboy, conveniently, was not there to ask. Perhaps a guest had picked it up by mistake.

I did not believe him. And it suddenly struck me, with chilling intensity, that in concern over my missing luggage I had become distracted from the more serious matter of a missing father. One thing was sure; I was not going to get help here.

"Very well," I said coldly. "*Mañana*. If the maids do not find my bag tomorrow morning, we will go to the police. Meanwhile I wish to telephone the nearest American consul about my bag, and about my father."

There were no phones, just bare wires, in the lobby telephone booths. The manager, with infinite courtesy, offered me the telephone in his office. I changed my mind quickly.

"No, thank you. I'll go up to town." Maybe I was being paranoid, but I had a sudden image of eavesdroppers listening to the conversation.

And I was suddenly very angry. Afraid and shaking and absolutely furious. The fury carried me out of the hotel, up the main road toward the center of town. It wasn't till I was a good way up the hill that I realized I had no idea of where I was going.

And there was no one to ask. Not here. Once beyond the hotel's lush grounds, I was in an area that was almost slum. Eyes peered at me, slyly or boldly, from rag-curtained doorways or rusty sidewalk tables, where there *was* sidewalk. Even the cobbled street was very narrow. There were boarded-up stores turned into living quarters or deserted. There was rubble where buildings once had been. A half-naked child, playing in the rubble, gave me a snag-toothed grin. The road along the shore had definitely been better. I didn't dare turn and go back there now. Or try to cut to it through the warren of

19

twisting alleys to my left. I didn't dare slow my pace or look uncertain. For suddenly I was very much afraid.

Not just of my surroundings. Afraid of the *slap-slap* of sandalled feet that had followed me inexorably the past three blocks. I willed myself not to turn, not to panic and run. I kept going doggedly, enormously glad that I had on dark glasses, that no one could see my eyes trying to catch a reflection of my follower in windows that I passed. A tall figure in white shirt and trousers, always a half a block behind.

I increased my pace imperceptibly, and he did also. The route came to an abrupt stop at a souvenir shop and angled right, up wide, iron-railed steps. Steps and steep walks and more steps zigzagged back and forth, up, up to the upper town. Vines and tropical flowers foamed from windowboxes and cascaded down the walls, and I kept going. My pace grew slower, and that of my sandalled follower did as well.

Coincidence, I told myself grimly, though I did not believe it. Or just someone following me because I'm a girl, and young. That was scary enough, but not as much so as the other possibilities coursing through my mind.

I ran around another turn, up the last steps, and was out at last onto a plaza. Beside me a church bell tolled the hour: four. My pursuer was not yet in sight. On sudden inspiration I ducked into the church, into a side pew, knelt quickly, throwing my black cardigan over my head so I would look like all the other black-shawled women. If he came in, the church was very dim. . . .

How long I knelt there I do not know; but when I rose, my knees were stiff and hurting, and the candle flames swam before my eyes. But no sandalled feet followed me as I walked through streets, now filled with a cooler light.

I found the main shopping street of Torremolinos, but no public phones. Then I found an elegant plaza, filled with cafes, and with telephones that I did not know how to use. And finally I found a luxury hotel, all Moorish architecture and tile and leather sofas, where a concierge speaking perfect British English told me how to call the nearest American consulate. I did not give him my reasons, and he did not ask.

The connection was bad. Or perhaps I was not making sense. I was aware now that I was very tired. The Consul General was not in his office. Whoever I spoke to thought I was making a fuss about nothing. I had my money, credit cards and passport? What did it matter if only some clothes and personal effects were gone? Reporting to the police would be a good idea, although they probably could not do much. Petty thievery in tourist resorts was so very common. As for my father, probably I had a made a mistake, or the manager had.

"We find, for reasons best known to themselves, many of these low-priced European hotels keep very poor records. Not much we can do about it, however." His tone was faintly amused, faintly deprecating. "Meanwhile, Miss—Langham, is it? I'd suggest you get a good night's sleep. Things will look better in the morning, and by then your father will quite likely have turned up." Yes, surely I could come in and file an official request for help if I needed it—*mañana*.

He didn't believe me, or at least didn't take me seriously. He didn't even recognize Gabriel Langham's name. So much for fame, I thought bitterly, heading toward the shore down those interminable stairs. This time I would follow the shore road.

Daylight was paling rapidly into twilight now. I walked and walked, my calves aching and the soles of my shoes feeling as though they were made of cardboard. I saw at last, blessedly, the rooftop sign of La Colomba. Five more blocks, or six, and I would be to the vacant lot with its short-cut path.

Here it was, the footpath with its rubble and its friendly goat. The rooster and his ladyfriends had vanished. I kept my eyes on the path, straining to make out stones in the gathering dimness. When a voice spoke, directly in front of me, I almost screamed.

"You have time?"

I stared, half paralyzed, at a slight, olive-skinned young man in shabby clothes. "Time?" he repeated. *"Hora?"*

Thank heaven my watch was pushed up my arm, hidden by the sleeve of my blouse! "No," I said shortly, and tried to cut past him. Swift as I was, he was even faster. He moved with lithe grace, like a cat, utterly relaxed; I noticed that even through my rising panic. With that one move he was blocking my path.

"American? *Turista*?" He smiled familiarly, and a gold tooth glinted. "Pretty girl should not be out alone—"

"There you are, my dear! Why didn't you wait for us?" I whirled, startled, as a woman's voice spoke directly at my shoulder. She was middle-aged and pleasant-faced, and I had never seen her before in my life. Yet she and the man with her smiled and nodded as if they were old friends. They closed in on either side of me, cutting me off from the young Spaniard, and all the time her matter-of-fact, slightly accented voice went on. "We will walk you back to the hotel, yes? My husband and I, we are going straight there, also. See, we have already reached the steps to the back garden."

So we had. They swept me along, as the Spaniard melted away into the shadows. She did not let go my arm until we reached La Colomba's pool, glimmering in the dusk. Then she turned to me, her face kind but stern. "I hope we did not frighten you. We saw you in the hotel lobby earlier, and just now we feared you might be in need of help. My dear, *never* go through that vacant field alone! My husband will not let me take that path, even with another woman, unless he is with me. There has been trouble there. Beggars, thieves—"

They insisted on escorting me to the elevator. They would have seen me clear to my room if I had let them. I was very grateful and very shaken; but despite my dread of it, I knew I needed to be alone. Too many things were whirling through my head, and I had to think.

Except I didn't. When I threw myself down on the bed, I sank at once, without any dinner, into an exhausted sleep.

3

I awoke wtih a splitting headache. Sunlight was pouring in unfamiliar windows, and there was a gnawing in my stomach. For a moment I lay there, all disoriented. Then with a rush, remembrance returned. Remembrance and alarm.

I showered, drying myself on the bedsheet since the bathroom still had neither soap nor towels. Then I pulled on a sedate blouse and chino skirt. Perhaps the peremptory treatment I'd received yesterday had been caused by my wearing jeans. After running a comb through my damp, dark hair, I surveyed myself hastily, wishing I looked older. Wishing I *felt* older and more assured. Then I grabbed my handbag and, holding onto it tightly, went downstairs.

I mean that literally. The elevator was not working. Twelve flights is a long way down, and on each level the corridors stretched out like spiders' legs, dimly lighted with a few bare bulbs. No wonder Dad hadn't stayed here, I thought, shivering. If he had ever been here!

I brought myself up short. My thinking was being affected by the manager's tale, and I must not let that happen. Dad could be here under another name; he could have been here under another name and left; or the manager could be lying. But Dad *had* been here. I held onto my letter, and my belief in it, like a talisman. I would watch in the lobby to see if Dad appeared, and I would report his absence to the police when I reported my missing bag.

But first I must wait until management had the maids search the rooms. If they really had them do it, I thought cynically, resolving to find out, in fractured French, from my friendly maid. Meanwhile, I discovered a breakfast room off the hotel lobby. The coffee was overboiled and bitter and the bread was stale, but I was hungry.

I found the manager and asked about the search. He shrugged. There were many rooms. The maids would look in each as they made the beds. It would take time.

Before that day was over, I was going to hate hearing about how much time things took, but I didn't know that yet. I looked for a place to sit and prepared to watch the lobby traffic for my father.

The only thing sittable was the marble ledge of the center planter, and soon I was evicted from that by a young girl who made it plain I was in the way of her washing the floor. She pointed me toward a *Sala Residencia*, where dark brown carpeting covered walls as well as floor. Modern abstract paintings hung above low, white leather sofas and pale blue velvet easy chairs. It was spacious, serene and beautiful. And empty. Or was till a man with a vacuum appeared and chased me out again. By then I'd gotten the message. There wasn't going to be any lobby traffic to watch. The place was like a morgue.

And I could sit still no longer with only my own thoughts for company. I went back to the desk, found no one there, and went to the pool. Here sunlight warmed the chill that had lodged inside my bones. A few bronzed collegians were showing off their dives, chattering cheerfully in French and Spanish. A young family was sunbathing and murmuring in some Scandinavian tongue. Beyond that the pool was ringed by senior citizens in a wildly varying assortment of clothes, sunshades and sunburns. How tickled Dad would be by all this. I could almost see his eyes twinkling, see the wheels going round in his head as he composed an affectionate but irreverent essay.

Dad.

The man at the consulate was right. The theft of a duffle bag, though it felt like a personal violation, was only a matter of missing clothes. But a missing person—

I dropped down on the grass, feeling myself shivering, and forced my head to clear. That was why I was so frantically, obsessively preoccupied with my missing luggage, wasn't it? Because, sick and angry as that made me feel, it was less terrible, less unthinkable, than the fact that Dad was missing.

Gabriel Langham was missing. Sarah Gabriel Langham's duffle bag was missing. Both of them vanished from Apartemento la Colomba, whose management denied knowledge of the former and responsibility for the latter. There had to be a connection; it was just too much coincidence to be believed. Too much coincidence that I had been followed up to town last night; that the hotel manager did not want me to see the police; that he had warned me I would be causing trouble, putting myself in danger.

The man with the gold tooth in the vacant lot, *he* had warned me too. Coincidence?

My teeth chattered, and the midday sun beat down with a blue-white glare. I lay back and closed my eyes and tried to think things through.

Dad was not where he had said he would be. That was the solid fact to hold onto in a whirling world. Dad had been here on a potentially explosive story; and he had gone off, or had been made to go off. All else was either related to that, or irrelevant.

Something icy cold and wet struck me. I sat up, startled. The college crowd had given up diving and was splashing in the pool. A dark girl in a hot pink bikini smiled apologetically and shrugged. A tall blond young man pulled himself up on the pool edge in front of me.

"Terribly sorry. I guess we got carried away." His voice was attractive, husky, with the faintest trace of perhaps a British accent. *He* was attractive, too. Even in the midst of my anxiety, I noticed that. Callie should see him, I thought with wild irrelevancy.

"It's all right. A little water won't hurt me," I gabbled, conscious that I was turning scarlet.

"A lot wouldn't either. The pool's great. Why don't you—" He broke off, staring at me intently. "Don't I know you from somewhere?"

"I don't think so." Surely, I would have remembered him.

"I'm sure we've met. I know your face." He was gazing at it now as if committing it to memory, and a prickle ran up my spine. "I'm Quent Robards. My folks own a vacation condo in that tower there. I'm here with friends on spring vacation. Look, aren't you going to at least tell me your name? Then maybe I'd remember—"

Any other time I'd have followed through. In the light of recent events, all I felt was panic. "You're making a mistake," I blurted through stiff lips, and fled.

When I reached the lobby, I leaned against the marble wall and waited for my heart to stop pounding. I was alone. He hadn't followed me. I must have been paranoid to think he would, to think there was something suspicious in his trying to scrape up an acquaintance.

But when the manager told me the maids had not yet finished their luggage check, I didn't go back to the pool. I went up to my room and shut and double-locked the door.

It wasn't till midafternoon that the maids finished doing the rooms. I knew that was true because it wasn't till then that my own room was done. The little maid whipped through the suite as quickly as possible, barely meeting my eyes. She didn't even give it what Selena would have called a "lick and a promise," and looked frightened when I tried again to speak to her in French. "*Beaucoup à faire,*" she mumbled, and I understood she was trying to tell me that she had no time.

I understood something else, too. She was trying to get away from me. She didn't want to be reminded of yesterday's conversation. "*Ma bagage?*" I said loudly. "*Avez-vous la cherché dans les autres chambres?*" She went on snapping the sheets up as though she hadn't heard.

Was she the maid for room 1327, I wondered. The

manager had explained with elaborate patience that the same few maids did all the floors. There was a picture of Dad and me, together, in my wallet. I pulled it out and thrust it before her.

"*Voici ma père. Avez-vous le vu ici?*"

To my shock, she almost gasped. "*Non, non! Señorita, por favore!*"

She hadn't even looked at the picture. She just bolted out of the suite just as I had bolted from the young man at the pool and from the man who seemed to be following me last night.

I put the chain on my door when she left, but I did not lock it. I left it ajar just a crack, just enough for me to watch the corridor, and when I saw her leave the last room and scurry into the elevator with her pail and broom, I waited ten minutes, and then I too went down.

The manager, for a wonder, was at the desk. Yes, the maids had finished. No, they had not found my bag. He had not expected it to be recovered, his tone implied; they had troubled to search just to pacify a hysterical girl. He hoped that now I realized it was folly to try to regain mislaid or stolen property. *Hope again*, I thought grimly, and reminded him of his promise to take me to the police.

"Unless you prefer I go without you," I finished. And, remembering the couple who had rescued me in the lot last night, added firmly, "Perhaps I can get some other guests to go with me. I understand there have been other thefts and annoyances, as well."

Oh, no. I must not think of that. If I was so quixotic as to want to deal with the police, he himself would escort me as soon as his assistant came to relieve him. I should go and relax myself. He waved vaguely toward the lounge. He would come for me when it was time.

"I'll wait here," I said firmly.

The wait was three-quarters of an hour, short by Spanish standards. It seemed longer. So did the ride to the police station, with the manager driving like a matador after a bull. The car smelled of strong European tobacco, and a tarnished crucifix dangled from the mirror. I clutched the edge of the seat and prayed.

I don't know what I expected. Our police station back home, or something out of old *Kojak*s or *Hill Street Blues*? The Torremolinos station was in a white stucco building in a non-tourist business district. I remember seeing a sign for a travel agency across the street, and a shoe repair. I remember that the light in the station had a pale green glow to it and that two shirt-sleeved patrolmen lounging near the entrance wore white.

The officer in charge had pomaded hair and a luxuriant mustache. He greeted the hotel manager like an old friend. There must have been an advance telephone conference, for when he turned to me he clearly knew why I was there. And thought it absurd; thought it suspicious; thought it everything the manager had said he would. That came over, loud and clear, even though the policemen spoke no English. All of a sudden, the air in the stuffy station felt electric.

I produced my passport. I recounted my arrival at La Colomba . . . with no reservation . . . to surprise my father. No, I had not yet seen my father. He did not seem to be there. The manager, translating all this into Spanish, shrugged. The police officer looked at me oddly.

I plodded doggedly through a cross-examination of my first hours at the hotel and my discovery that one bag was missing. A part of my brain whispered in outrage, "This is crazy! I'm the victim, not the guilty party!" Another part, the part that was "Gabriel's girl," warned me to stay calm.

It all felt, crazily, like a reenactment of something I had been through already. I had, hadn't I? Yesterday, with the manager—the same wary disbelief that I could hold anyone else responsible for my own "carelessness," the suspicion as to the contents of the duffle. Have you ever tried to remember what you packed, in a hurry, in a given suitcase? With a sickening lurch I remembered that Mother's gold locket had been in it. Lord knows why I'd brought it—a wanting to believe that I'd find Dad quickly, that my fears were unfounded, that we'd be going together someplace where I could dress up? Now the locket, with its pictures of Mother and Dad when they were young, was gone, and my eyes filled suddenly with tears.

When the list was finished, the manager translated it for the policeman. Nothing on it was of great value; I understood that comment even before it was translated. Was I still determined to file an official report? I was. He typed it out, slowly, glancing at me from time to time as though it were an arrest form rather than a claim for property. Then I had to sign it! An official police paper on which I couldn't read a word! That jolted me, and the two men knew it. I saw them exchange glances and felt at an alarming disadvantage. And then, fiercely angry.

"About my father. *Mio padre*," I said loudly.

If I could report missing luggage, I could report a missing father. And I was not going out of there until I did. I don't know the moment my mind became made up; it simply was. Subtly, but definitely, the energy in the room shifted. I felt the way I did in a gymnastics contest, when I'd briefly wavered but then recovered balance and knew I was secure. Whether they felt it, too, or whether they were affected by the fact that doors and windows were open and I was talking loudly, I can't be sure, but suddenly the officer and hotel manager were taking the matter of Gabriel Langham seriously.

I went all through the business about room 1327 again. I hauled out Dad's now-wrinkled letter. How the officer was going to read Dad's cryptic English I did not know, but he could see the room number, the La Colomba letterhead, the name and address on the envelope the same as on my passport. I had come to surprise my father, I said, not telling my real reason, hoping I was not jeopardizing Dad's project by what I was doing.

Then staccato Spanish between the officer and the hotel manager. Then the officer on the telephone, with more rapid Spanish. Then, after a long interval, the manager turning to me decisively.

"Señorita, the lieutenant has been in touch with the agency of immigration. They have checked the United States of America passport records. No Gabriel Langham has entered Spain in the past month."

"But he did," I answered doggedly.

Another exchange of glances. The manager, carefully patient. "Señorita, I beg of you to consider. How could your father enter the country without a passport?"

The meaning beneath his words stood up and shouted at me. *Only if he entered the country illegally . . . without passing through immigration, or with forged credentials.*

In a momentary blackness, Callie's voice danced in my ears. *"CIA . . . I told you so. . . ."* Only it wasn't anything so legitimate that I read in the policeman's eyes.

For a moment, God help me, I wavered. For a moment I wanted to run and hide. Then something beyond myself took over. I heard my own voice say coldly, "There is some mistake. I will take it up with our ambassador." And I walked out of there with my head up, without a sign of trembling, and seated myself in the manager's car.

He was no help. The Spanish police were no help. Because Dad *was* in Spain, and if Gabriel Langham had not officially entered, then something was askew and I would have to find him on my own. And I knew, with a certainty beyond reason, that I would do so.

That was the first moment I began to realize perhaps I truly was Gabriel's girl.

4

When we reached the hotel again, tea was in progress. Clouds of cigarette smoke rose from tables where elderly Frenchwomen were playing bridge. Or French-Canadian —I heard references to "St. Laurent" and "Quebec" pop out of their staccato chatter as I passed. Well-behaved European children sat with their parents, paper napkins spread carefully in their laps. It was an odd assortment of guests, but no one, to be blunt, no one who was in Dad's age group or type. And no one who looked like a crook. I wondered, not for the first time, what had brought Dad here. The fact that it had been advertised on radio as a good buy suddenly seemed, knowing Dad, just too simple.

An attractive blonde Spanish woman was dispensing tea. I accepted a cup and an arrowroot cookie. The surge of adrenalin that had carried me out of the police station had subsided, leaving me shaky and very conscious of being seventeen, in a foreign country all alone. I wasn't ready yet to face the emptiness of that room upstairs. But nearly all the chairs and sofas were occupied by established groups, and I felt queer about intruding.

34

Then a woman caught my eye, smiled and beckoned. It was the lady from the vacant lot. I went over gratefully.

"And so how are you after your alarm? My husband and I, we were worried about you. We are Mr. and Mrs. Gustavsen, from Trondheim, Norway." Mr. Gustavsen rose, and we all shook hands formally.

"I'm—Sarah Gabriel. From New Jersey." The memory of what the police lieutenant had said leaped to my mind, and I held back the "Langham" just in time. If Dad was in this country, it was illegally. It would be best not to mention his name.

"You are here with your parents? Your grandparents?" Mrs. Gustavsen patted the seat beside her.

"No. I came alone." They looked shocked, and I added quickly, "I came to visit a relative. My—Uncle Ted." That was Dad's middle name, which he hated, so it wasn't likely anyone who knew of Gabriel Langham, author, knew about it. I fished in my wallet for the photograph, and the Gustavsens bent their heads above it.

"Why yes, of course." Mrs. Gustavsen flashed me a reassuring smile, and I sat up straight.

"You mean you've see him?"

"Last week. Is that not right, Oskar? We shared the elevator once or twice." Her eyes twinkled. "He has a camera bag with many gadgets on it, yes?"

"Yes!" The cup and saucer were starting to clatter in my hand. I put them on the table quickly. "When did you last see him? The—the front desk doesn't seem to know anything about him."

"The front desk!" Mrs. Gustavsen snorted. "Those young men know no more about running a hotel than babies. They have only taken over the hotel this year, you know."

"I wondered why things seemed so—inconsistent," I said carefully.

Mr. Gustavsen shook his head, displeased. "You are too kind. They are a disaster. When we were here four years ago, everything was as it should be. *Better* than it should have been. The hotel's founders went bankrupt two years ago."

He pointed toward the other high-rise buildings. "You see those? Beautiful! Privately owned condominiums by the same builder. That was what the *hotel* was like then. But these new owners?" He glanced around the lobby sadly. "No training, not enough money, not enough staff. So many of these old people, they put up with the inconveniences because the price is low. But us, we will not come again. Not even any telephone, you have seen? The government owns the telephone system in this country. The bureaucrats will not restore service here until the previous owners' bills are paid."

That could explain a lot, aboveboard or otherwise. Was it too much exposure to Callie, or to my father, that made me instantly wonder if these suave, inexperienced hotelkeepers were using La Colomba for something sinister? I said carefully, "The last time you saw my uncle—what was he doing?"

Her brow knotted. "Yes, of course. He rode into town on the same bus with us. The day I went to the shoemaker. Six days ago."

My heart was pounding. "Did he have luggage with him?"

"No. My dear, surely you do not think he would

leave Torremolinos if you were coming?"

"It was to be a surprise," I said through dry lips. "Are you sure you haven't seen him since?"

Mrs. Gustavsen shook her head, disturbed. Mr. Gustavsen said firmly, "We would have seen, if he had checked out. You know? He would fly to his next destination, yes? Few planes a day fly out of Malaga. And this place is inefficient. There is always great—what do you call it? Hubbub." He pointed to the lobby, where an army of suitcases and their impatient owners waited. "Always the delay for the check-out, for the taxis. If your uncle was there, we would have seen him."

"You know what maybe he did?" Mrs. Gustavsen said brightly. "There was a bus tour that went to the Algarve. Señora Rojas, the social hostess, arranged it. Many hotel guests have gone on that. They will return in a few days. You will be wise to wait and see if your uncle is among them."

"Yes, you're right." I was grasping at straws, but at least that provided a respectable reason for remaining at La Colomba. I forced myself to smile and look relieved. "I will—wait here. Mrs. Gustavsen, do you know a good restaurant where I could have dinner?" Thank goodness I had enough money with me. There was at least a chance I might run into my father if I went where the food was good.

"You should not go out alone." Mr. Gustavsen was emphatic. "In Spain, it is not proper for young women, and you would ask for trouble. Tonight we are going with a group to a flamenco club. Why do you not join us? Señora Rojas, who is pouring the tea, will arrange it."

The club was stucco-walled and dim and, like everywhere else I'd been, filled with tobacco smoke. Dad wasn't there. Dad wouldn't have thought much of the beef that Sra. Rojas raved about. But the gazpacho and paella were good, the guitar music and folk singing was hypnotic, and the flamenco dancers wove a spell. Tucked into a banquette between the Gustavsens and a grand-motherly Brooklyn lady, I could almost relax and con-vince myself that this was an ordinary (by Langham ex-perience, anyway) vacation. Almost, but not quite.

It was eleven before the flamenco display began. In the darkness, I could sense additional parties still arriv-ing. The restaurant was crowded now. After the flamenco dancers took a flamboyant bow and swept out for an in-termission, the lights in the overhead lanterns came up slightly. Couples began to fill the postage-stamp-sized dance floor. Mr. Gustavsen led his wife to it sedately.

"You should be dancing," Mrs. Levitz said to me. I shook my head.

"I'd rather sit. Really."

"Nonsense, you're too young to be out with a bunch of old fogies like us. There's a bunch of young folks from the La Colomba condominiums at that other table. Why don't you just go introduce yourself?" I looked up, alarmed, as she chuckled and added, "Guess you won't have to!"

Coming toward me was the golden-haired young man from the swimming pool.

"Would you like to dance?" he asked.

"No," I said. "No, thank you." I was blushing, and I knew he knew it. His gray eyes twinkled.

"Oh, come on. Even if I can't remember your name. I won't bite you."

"Her name's Sarah," the Brooklyn lady volunteered, beaming. "Go ahead, dearie. He's a nice boy. I've seen him around the pool a lot." She obviously thought she was doing a good deed, encouraging me. And her voice was loud. I was dying with embarrassment, and he knew that, too. His face tried to remain properly serious, but his eyes danced.

Oh, why not, I thought recklessly. I'm safe enough here, I'm with a group. And I took his hand and let him lead me to the floor.

He danced well. Certainly none of the boys I knew at home could have danced like that to Latin music and managed to make me look good, too. When the violin slowed into a haunting love song, I found myself melting in his arms. It was the melody and the atmosphere of this place and my own weariness; it was all that, and other things I did not want to face as well.

"Sarah," he murmured against my hair. "Just Sarah?"

"Mm-hmm." Even as vulnerable as I was, something told me not to speak my name.

I could feel him laughing at me gently. "All right, Sarah No-Name. The crowd's going to go on to a jazz club that's not quite as senior citizenish as this place. Why don't you come?"

"I can't."

"Oh, come on. You know who I am, which is more than I know about you. I swear to you that somewhere or other we were properly introduced. I'm a Canadian citizen, my dad's in the diplomatic corps, I go to Oxford, I'm clean-living, upright and loyal to queen and country. I used to be a Boy Scout. I'll even promise not to make a pass at you, if you insist."

"I can't. Really." Involuntarily I glanced back at the banquette where the Gustavsens were now watching me anxiously, and he followed my glance. "Parents? Chaperones? All right, I won't ask. But you're not getting rid of me as easily as that, Sarah No-Name."

There was a roll of drums, the lights flickered, and the dance floor cleared as the flamenco artists reappeared. Quent escorted me back to my seat with a flourish, bowed and took his leave.

Quent. Quent Robards. I had remembered his name, when I had no reason to. I answered the Gustavsens' questions bemusedly and sat through the flamenco number in a daze.

When the show was over, Sra. Rojas appeared. If our group wished, she would take us on to one or two other, smaller clubs, where we could hear the celebrated gypsy "deep-song" singers. Sherry, brandy, coffee or soft drinks could be purchased. There was no obligation. The van driver waited to take those who wished to end the evening now back to La Colomba.

There was a flurry of activity and conferring. The Gustavsens wanted to retire. I needed sleep, but I dreaded returning to La Colomba and that empty room. At last my self-appointed guardians decided I would be safe enough with the group and with Mrs. Levitz as my chaperone. We gathered up our things and edged out into the Spanish night.

The moon was like a huge lantern, and the air was cool and heady with Mediterranean herbs and flowers. Sra. Rojas led our party by foot through streets that were scarcely more than narrow alleys.

Again, a low-ceilinged stucco room with dark wood and haunting music. Again, the sick-sweet smoke. Again, a tall blond young man coming across the room toward me and smiling.

I stared, blinked, shook my head slightly, but he was still there, pulling up a chair and winking at Mrs. Levitz, who beamed with satisfaction. "I thought you were going to a jazz club," I managed at last.

"I was. Until I found out through classified sources you were going someplace better." Quent grinned at Mrs. Levitz. "So I ditched the others and came on here. Clever of me, wasn't it?"

Too clever. I couldn't believe he had followed me just because of my fatal fascination. I didn't like the things I was imagining—or feeling, either.

I sipped a too-sweet lemonade and sank into silence. Presently, Sra. Rojas began stirring us to our feet again. More walking, more narrow streets, steeply downhill into a poorer part of town. We passed a painted-out window with a faded sign, *"Carniceria,"* and I was thrown back to that first hot afternoon when I had been followed beneath a blazing sun. I kept up with the group doggedly, not looking in Quent's direction. Had it just been my paranoid imagination or had that man in white been following me? And if so, why, and who? He had been tall, but he had worn a hat so I had not been able to see the color of his hair—

The realization of what I was thinking struck me like a blow. It was ridiculous. Fantastic. But nonetheless I managed in the darkness to separate myself from Quent. But the chill, queasy feeling of being followed persisted.

I stumbled on a loose cobblestone, lost balance and

brought myself up against a cracked stucco wall. No one saw. It was so dark, and the others were moving on, laughing. I righted myself, took a deep breath and turned round instinctively to look back down the street before hurrying on.

Not two yards away a figure watched me in the shadows. He moved slightly, and moonlight glinted on a gold tooth.

I couldn't move. For a moment, literally, I could not move.

"Sarah, are you all right?" Quent was at my elbow. "The others are getting ahead, you'd better hurry—" He stopped, looked at me sharply and slid an arm around me. "You're not all right. You're shaking with chill."

"I'm just very tired."

"Want me to take you home?"

"No." I tried to straighten, but my legs would not cooperate. The gold-toothed man had vanished.

"I'll get a cab and take both you and Mrs. Levitz back. Her feet are giving out on her." By now he knew not just her name but those of her five grandchildren as well. Before I knew what was happening, I was in the back seat of a cab next to Mrs. Levitz, with Quent turned round in the front seat so he could face us.

At La Colomba, Mrs. Levitz, torn between wanting to hover and wanting to be tactful, kissed me, murmured her room number to me and made for the elevator. Quent looked at me.

"You really are exhausted, aren't you? Want me to see you upstairs?"

"No—thank you." I skittered toward the elevator just as the door slid shut in my face.

"Aren't you going to collect your key?"

"I have it." I hadn't trusted leaving it at the desk, and I didn't want Quent to know my room number now. If only Mrs. Levitz wasn't such a matchmaker! I wished passionately that she had waited, that I'd had the nerve to ask if I could stay in her apartment that night. Which was I more afraid of, going up into that empty, echoing corridor alone or going there with Quent? I did not know, any more than I knew the reason for my fear. It was simply there. When the man behind the reception counter called out to me, I almost screamed.

"Senorita." He was holding out an envelope. I had to walk over and take it, walk back to the elevator, under Quent's very close and very watchful eye.

"Aren't you even curious what your mail is?" he asked.

"No." I jammed it into my purse as if it was of no importance. It almost burned my fingers, but I could not, would not open it with him there. And then the elevator door opened; I got on and pushed my hand down hard and quick on the floor button. The doors slammed together, cutting him from view.

The elevator groaned upward. Its one ceiling light bulb was very dim. I clutched my purse against my hammering heart, and at last the doors opened onto my floor and I was running, running down the dark corridors while the pulse pounded like thunder in my ears.

My fingers fumbled with the door key. Then I was inside, the door was shut and bolted, the room's inadequate ceiling light was on. I dumped the contents of my purse out on the bed, snatched up the envelope and tore it open.

Its content was a single sheet.

If you want to see the bad
penny again, go home at once
and wait for further word.

The printing was not familiar. The paper was plain pale gray. Plain, cheap white paper was the envelope, and it had no stamp, no return address. No proper address, either, just two typed words. *Sarah Langham*. For once, not Sarah *Gabriel* Langham, I thought numbly.

I sat on the hard bed, in the ceiling lamp's gray circle of light, staring at the message for a long, long time.

5

When I awoke, shivering, to a cold morning light, a few things stood out sharp and clear. Dad had certainly not gone to the Algarve, and he was in trouble. I was not going to get help from the Spanish police. I was not going to get help from La Colomba. It was up to me.

One word leaped into my mind. *Madrid*. The American Embassy was in Madrid, and Tom McLean was at the Embassy. *He* would do something. And could tell me what to do.

I dressed, packed my bags and went downstairs carrying them with me.

"I am going to Madrid about my father," I told the desk man crisply. "I may be gone a day, perhaps more. I wish to leave my suitcase in your baggage room until I return."

I had a qualm about doing that, but I didn't want to drag it with me—not just because it would be a nuisance, but because it would look as if I were quitting the field. It could be important for it to be known that I was not giving up my search in Torremolinos. And I had a strong feeling that leaving my suitcase in the luggage room was less risky than leaving it in my room. At least, that was what the manager had insisted when blaming me for carelessness earlier.

The manager was not pleased. He also, to my utter astonishment, remarked coldly that it was "inadvisable for one to go about spreading libelous rumors."

"I beg your pardon?" I said blankly.

"The Norwegian gentleman and lady. My associate heard you repeating to them your unfounded accusations."

I felt stunned, then furious, and said something about "eavesdropping on private conversations." Then I took the baggage receipt he handed me and got out of there. I didn't even stop to have breakfast. I went out the front door, down to the main highway, waited with a German family for a bus to come, then boarded it and rode into town.

How I would get to Madrid I did not know, but there had to be a bus or train or *something* out of Torremolinos. For some reason I couldn't put my finger on, I didn't want to use the credit card and fly. Something kept saying to me that the less I was identified as Gabriel Langham's daughter, the better. Anyway, Madrid was only a few hours away.

I got off the bus at the Torremolinos main drag, feeling safer for the crowds around me. I found the train station. Yes, there was a train, but not for another two hours. I found the bus station. The bus left sooner, but would get to Madrid later. I settled for the train.

The train ticket took almost all my Spanish money, and it occurred to me that I had better get more changed.

There were banks all over the place. I had plenty of time, enough time to stop in a cafe and have a pastry and coffee first. I did have enough pesos for that.

I found the square that I had seen before, found a cafe where the pastries behind the window glass appealed to me, sat down at an outside table. Said "*Galletas*," and "*cafe*," and "*con leche*," as automatically as if I were ordering a hamburger and Coke somewhere at home. I saw my reflection in the window glass, and I looked so calm. I *was* calm, that was what was so queer. It was as if I was standing off watching myself, in a dream. Or nightmare.

And all the while the events of the past days hung at the edge of consciousness, like a gathering storm.

The coffee came, and I drank it. I ate the pastry, which was delicious, scattering powdered sugar all over my flounced denim skirt. Then still feeling curiously dreamlike, I brushed myself off and crossed the square to the *Banco Popular*.

There were two men ahead of me in the line at the window for foreign exchange. The second man had problems, which he went into at great length in angry Spanish. I remember noticing how red his neck got and how beads of sweat stood out on it. At some point, I became aware of a woman in black getting into line behind me. I remember surreptitiously fishing inside the waistband of my skirt, locating the U.S. bills that, following Dad's precaution in pickpocket areas, I had stashed inside my underwear. I remember congratulating myself on having had the sense not to have carried either money, credit cards or passport in my duffle. Then the man in front completed his transaction in a huff, and it was my turn.

I pushed my money through the slot beneath the glass barrier.

"Passport," the teller said without looking up.

"But they're not travelers' checks. They're bills."

The teller shrugged. "Passport," he repeated flatly. So much for anonymity, I thought, digging for the navy-blue booklet and passing it through quickly. The teller copied the number, gave the picture and me a cursory glance and thrust passport, money and receipt back through the glass.

It happened so quickly that at first I did not know what was going on.

One minute I was scooping my belongings up out of the green marble hollow in the counter. The next I felt a quick, sharp jerk. Then I was staring, dumbly, at a wad of colored bills and a handful of coins.

The money was there. The passport was gone.

Staccato exclamations broke out around me. "These pickpockets! It has become too much!" A well-dressed woman behind me added a terse, emphatic term in Spanish. "Senorita, I apologize for my city. Are you all right?"

Another man was already running toward the door. "No use," the teller called. "She was too quick. By now she'll have vanished down an alley."

"I don't understand," I heard my own voice say dazedly. "My money—the money's still here."

"Money!" The teller at the next window snorted. "These days, what is money? It was the *Estados Unidos* passport that was wanted. There is—how you say? A profitable black market. These pickpocket rings are *muy mundano*. Assuredly, that woman was a part of one."

"Woman?"

"The old woman who stood between us. That is who it was. She must have recognized you as *Americano* and followed you in." The lady behind me smiled reassuringly. "Do not be so alarmed, Señorita. You have your money. The passport you report to the police, and they will tell your consulate and see that it is replaced. You have nothing to fear."

"Not the police," I said sharply. I swept the money into my purse and strode out, leaving heaven knew what reactions in my wake. I was starting to shake. And I was starting to laugh.

Nothing to fear. A pickpocket ring. Criminal ring. After *a* U.S. passport, or *my* passport? Out in the square, I made it past three stores before I leaned against a marble wall and laughed until I was bent double and my stomach hurt.

Why had I not looked at that woman when I sensed someone behind me? I would at least have known if she was someone I had seen before. Here in town, or at the hotel.

I could almost hear the police laughing at me, if I were even able to make them understand the story. Madrid. I must get to Madrid and find Uncle Tom, lay it all before him. He could take care of the passport, tell me where he'd seen Dad and what Dad had said. Tell me what to do.

"I'll tell you what to do," Tom McLean said with kind firmness. "Go back home before father tries to phone you, gets no answer and goes out of his skull with worry."

"But I can't—"

"Of course, you can. You got yourself over here, didn't you? I'll take care of getting a new passport issued." Uncle Tom's eyes twinkled. "Don't you dare quote me, but a lost passport isn't as much of a deal as the Passport Office would like you to believe."

"How can you *say* that? Especially when it wasn't *lost*—"

"OK, OK, stolen. Your bank acquaintance was right about there being a black market. But I will say not to worry. The computer system will check your passport number and report it to every U.S. immigration office. Nobody's going to slip into the States claiming to be you."

"That's not what I'm worrying about!" My voice was getting shrill. Uncle Tom and I had been talking for half an hour, and that half-hour had shown me a Tom McLean I'd never known before. Or, rather, shown how he saw *me*.

About my train ride earlier from Torremolinos, the less said the better. When I got to Madrid I was still half numb, half shaking. I kept my "international traveler" façade till I got past the embassy's radar screen, past the Marine guards, down the rabbit-warren of corridors to Uncle Tom's office. But once inside, looking into his friendly freckled face, I have to admit it, I just went to pieces. He got me coffee and closed the door so the two of us were alone. And I poured out the story, all of it, from the moment I'd tried to phone Dad from home and was told he wasn't there.

When I finished at last, I was exhausted. And Uncle Tom was looking at me with a faint smile on his face. Looking *amused*.

He was still looking that way now, after I'd spent

fifteen minutes trying to make him take Dad's disappearance seriously. He wasn't exactly laughing at me, it was more the way a proud parent looks at a precocious child.

"I don't see how you can take this so lightly!" I burst out. "I thought Dad was your best friend! Didn't he say *anything* to you when he saw you about where he was going or what he was working on?"

"Since when would Gabe Langham give away leads on a story?" Uncle Tom asked patiently. "Even to me, even if I should see him."

I looked pointedly at Dad's letter to me, which lay on his desk next to last night's disturbing note. Uncle Tom followed my glance, and to give him credit, his own expression sobered. He swung his feet to the floor and leaned forward toward me.

"Sorry, Sarah. I didn't mean to seem callous. Or patronizing. It's just that you threw me a curve coming out with those suspicions. Over twenty-five years I've gotten used to Gabe's hair-raising imagination, scenting espionage and intrigue in every corner. I just wasn't expecting it of his daughter." He held his hand up quickly. "Don't start getting your dander up again. If I'm not worried, it's because I know no reason to be. For Pete's sake, Sarah, you know what Gabe's like!"

"I know that nine times out of ten when he smells a rat somewhere, there *is* a rat."

"And that tenth time he's called out the heavy-duty exterminators for nothing. And of the other nine, maybe half are pretty small mice. At the very most, not warranting the big mystery smokescreen Gabe's thrown up around the chase." Tom McLean grinned. "I've got to admit, though, it sure sells a lot of books. And before you get mad, no, I don't think that's why your father does it. I think he does it because he thrives on the excitement. Sitting in an ivory tower with a typewriter would be too tame for a guy with his background."

"You mean he's missing his work with the CIA?"

"For heaven's sake, don't dig up that old chestnut!"

"He's never satisfactorily buried it, and you know it."

"If you want to know what I think, that's because he gets a big bang out of it. 'A hero to his kid,' you know?" Uncle Tom chuckled, but his eyes were kind. "Look, Sarah, I know you're really worried, but take my word for it, you needn't be. Go on back to the States, and I'll bet you'll be hearing his voice on the telephone next Sunday night. When you do, tell him to give me a call, the son of a gun. I haven't had a good jaw with him in ages. And don't start insisting again that I just saw him. The fact that he knows I'm stationed here doesn't mean we were in touch."

He reached for the telephone. "I'll get my secretary started on the paperwork for your new passport. Your duffle bag, I'm afraid, is gone for good. Torremolinos is a notorious tourist trap, meaning there are a lot of petty thieves who grab what they can, keep whatever can be quickly fenced and discard the rest. We can go through the motions with the local police, but don't expect results."

"What about 'going through the motions' with the hotel manager, who insisted Dad was never there and then gave me that note last night?"

Something changed in his eyes then. But not his voice; it was still lightly matter-of-fact. "I don't like the sound of that place one bit. Not for cloak-and-dagger reasons, but because it doesn't sound like any fit place for a young girl alone. Come to think of it, you'd better stay here with us. Lydia will love it; she hasn't seen you for two years. It'll take several days for the passport to come through, and Gabe would kill me if we let you wait them out on the Costa del Sol alone."

Uncle Tom rose. "Unfortunately I've got a meeting in five minutes, and Lydia won't be home till dinnertime. But you can give Miss Stevens all the information for the forms and wait for me in the embassy library. Tell her she's to make arrangements to have your luggage brought here from that dive you left it at. And stop worrying, sweetie. It's ninety-nine and forty-four/one hundredths percent certain that note's a joke. But if it isn't, you'll be exactly where it says for you to be—at home."

He went to his meeting. I put the note and letter in my purse and went out to Miss Stevens, where I answered all the questions she asked me for the passport. However, I didn't tell her to arrange about my luggage, and I told her that the directions she gave me to the library were so clear she needn't go down with me.

Actually, I didn't go there myself, either. I went to the nearest exit door and out into the street. I still felt cold, but in other ways I was numb, not even hungry, although my lunch had consisted of two breadsticks and nothing more. And I wasn't staying in Madrid. If no one, not even Uncle Tom, was about to look for Dad, it was clearly up to me.

6

Stupidly, I had not asked what times trains ran back to Torremolinos. It was now late in the day, and the thought of that return journey, alone through darkness, filled me with dread. *Everything* filled me with dread. Cold and weakness had taken up permanent residence in my stomach.

"Stop this," I told myself sternly. Now if ever, I had to behave like Gabe Langham's daughter. Which did not involve feeling queasy or wishing—as I did passionately—that someone would come along, take over and remove the burden from my shoulders. "What would Dad do now?" I asked myself, and the answer came clearly. Not waste time hitting his head against stone walls. Analyze the evidence; regroup; look for trails under, over or around the aforesaid walls (meaning Uncle Tom, the police, the hotel manager). Losing battles did not mean losing the war. What general was it who'd said, "Retreat, hell! I'm just advancing in another direction!"

My mind skittered uneasily away from the war imagery, but it persisted. I had to think before I did any more dashing off from anger or from panic, and first I had to clear my head. On the theory that there was safety in numbers, I sat down at a crowded outdoor cafe and ordered *tapas*—snacks—and bitter chocolate. Then deliberately, as I had seen Dad do when seeking the structure for a story, I laid the disparate clues out in my mind.

Fact: Dad had said he was staying at la Colomba, and the managers insisted that he wasn't. Fact: for some reason he hadn't wanted me to call him there. (Why? Alias?)

Fact: he was on the trail of something big. (Query: dangerous? Query: was that fact hearsay?)

Fact: nobody wanted me in Torremolinos—not Uncle Tom, not the hotel management. (Query: why? All the more reason for me to go back there?) Fact: enough unpleasantnesses were happening to drive me from there. (Coincidence?) Fact: no one was taking me or my complaints/demands/worries seriously. They thought I was hysterical. They thought I was a suspicious character. They thought Dad was.

Fact: nobody was going to do a darn thing to help. In fact they were doing exactly the opposite. (Or was that my imagination? Paranoia?)

Fact: I had been followed. By two different persons, I had been followed. No matter how Uncle Tom tried to brush that off. . . .

I gazed across the plaza over the rim of the chocolate cup, my face flushing at the memory of Tom McLean's amused half-smile. Then my fingers froze around the cup handle.

On a bench by a flowerbed in the center of the plaza a slight, dark Spaniard was looking at me above a newspaper. *It can't be*, reason told me, but I recognized the lines of the wiry body, the tilt of the head, the glint of gold tooth before the concealing paper went up quickly.

A paper . . . a Spanish beggar reading a paper? But I had never believed he was a beggar, had I? There are hundreds of Spaniards with rumpled white clothes and gold teeth, reason insisted. It couldn't be the man from Torremolinos. But another part of my brain swore back, *It could.*

With fingers suddenly clumsy, I put coins carefully on the table, rose as unobtrusively as possible and, threading close to the cafe building, began to make my way along the plaza. There was no reason for a man engrossed in a newspaper to notice me. Yet, when I had gone half a block, I saw him, reflected in the window glass, fold his paper and saunter after me. I accelerated my pace; he did also.

The now-familiar panic came welling up in me again. I forced myself to stay calm and think clearly. Surely, nothing could happen to me in broad daylight in a crowd. That was it; I must stay with people. And preferably lose myself among them. When a street vendor went by, his cart blocking me from view, I ducked into a women's wear shop and spent what seemed an eternity browsing among the racks of dresses at the back.

When I came out again, the late sun was slanting. The figure in rumpled whites was lounging against a shop entry across the plaza, half-hidden by a rack of picture postcards.

I don't know if he knew I saw him. I had that much advantage, at least. But the plaza was emptying now, as people went home before preparing for the Spanish night. Quite suddenly, the full weight of being in Madrid alone, without a passport, descended on me. Had the last train gone? How could I register in a hotel here without a passport? I cursed myself for carelessness.

I could go to Uncle Tom's, reason reminded me. There lay safety and being taken care of and a return to adolescence. There lay the end of any hope of searching for Dad. All these thoughts clicked through my brain as I was moving methodically, deliberately casual, toward the railroad station. And my white shadow moved with me. I dared not turn my head, but I kept his reflection in my gaze as he followed me.

The streets were growing more deserted. There were two blocks I would have to pass through, narrow, with blank walls and a few high windows. That, if anywhere, was where I could be most vulnerable. The computer in my head clicked out this information as my mind raced frantically, searching for a way out. And my feet kept moving, closer and closer toward the dreaded passage.

A voice said, "Fancy meeting you here," and I almost screamed.

Quent. Quent, appearing out of nowhere again. He was not in beach attire now, but wore proper city clothes. And his eyes were twinkling, as his hands caught mine.

"This time I'm not going to let you get away. Because, by heaven, I've finally remembered!" He held me still, stopped me, so that my follower was almost upon us before realizing it and vanishing into a doorway. But Quent didn't see. He was looking straight at me, blue eyes triumphant.

"I knew we'd met somewhere! It was the Canadian embassy in Washington, and you had on a bright green dress. It was some kind of summer reception, and you were there because your father and mine are old diplomatic corps friends. You're Sarah Gabriel Lang—"

"*Stop it!*" My voice, thank God, was a whisper, though it came with all the vehemence of a shout. Involuntarily my head swerved around, toward that seemingly empty doorway. And my fingers must have tightened around his, for suddenly he was very still. Suddenly his arm was sliding around me, casually, as if he were any American boy walking with his girlfriend. His voice was casual, too, saying with light laughter, "Okay, let's can it for now. We can talk when we get to my dad's place." Innocuous words, but the pressure on my arm tightened as he said them, and I remembered suddenly that his "dad's place" of business was the Canadian Embassy.

Quent was flagging a cab. I had only seconds to decide. A cab made a U-turn with a screech of brakes, and mistrust and trust hung in the balance.

I got into the cab.

Quent slid in quickly and slammed the door. "Toward the Cathedral," he ordered the driver crisply, and then turned to me. "Dad's office or the house, which would you rather? My folks are out, but I guarantee you our housekeeper Ascension is the soul of propriety."

I came to a swift decision. "House." I had had enough of Embassies. Quent gave the driver an address, and during the rest of the short trip we rode in silence. I had sunk into a curious exhaustion. It was as if, in coming with Quent, I had made some irrevocable decision that lightened the weight on my shoulders.

We came to a stately, whitewashed villa and went inside. It was cool and quiet; it seemed empty until a stout, pleasant-faced Spanish matron stepped from a corridor. "Señora Ascension Moreno," Quent said formally, and she nodded. I nodded back, noticing that he did not supply my name. He had grasped my alarm over its use.

He steered me into a long salon with modern leather chairs and sofas and turned back toward the door. "Open or shut?"

"Shut." I was past worrying about propriety, or about my safety with him. What mattered was Dad's safety; and when Quent, having closed the door, looked at me across that expanse of polished tile and said, "All right, what's wrong?" I told him.

"Gabe's disappeared." That was all I could say at first, but Quent looked neither shocked nor doubting. He did not rush me. I found myself sitting on the arm of a chair and telling him the story, all of it, everything that had happened in those incredible past days. Gradually, the account gained form and sharpness by his quiet questions.

When I had finished, there was a silence. Quent rang a bell and then crossed to the door. I was in the chair by now, and I leaned back and closed my eyes, wondering what he was thinking. He must have given Ascension quiet orders, for presently he came back and thrust a tall, cold glass of orange juice into my hand. Then he sat down across from me and said, as if it were the most natural thing in the world, "All right, let's see what we should do first."

I sat up straight. "*We?*"

"Of course. You are a friendly neighbor who's come for assistance to a representative of the Canadian government, aren't you?" Quent grinned. "Unfortunately the official government representative, namely my father, is

59

back in Ottawa at the moment. But as a member of his family I do have diplomatic immunity and a fair amount of pull. And I definitely think it's time for some North American cooperative effort. You're right, you're getting a royal runaround. I recognize the signs."

"So do I." I was still smarting from Uncle Tom's reaction. "What I don't understand," I said slowly, "is why. I'm afraid I can guess the hotel people's reasons. But why won't our own embassy take it seriously?"

" 'Why' isn't relevant, unless it has bearing on the reasons for your father's vanishing. Which it may; we'll get to that in time. First thing is to follow up on his last known appearance." Quent narrowed his eyes. "He was seen getting on a bus with his camera bag, you say. What happened to his other luggage?"

"I never thought of that!" I could have kicked myself.

"Something else we'll have to look into at the hotel." He reached for the telephone. "Just thought of something I *can* check for you from here," he murmured, dialing. "Mr. Wittington? Quent Robards . . . Fine, thanks. Look, sir, I just found out a good friend of my dad's is supposed to be in the country. Gabriel Langham . . . That's right, the author." Quent frowned ferociously as I straightened. "I know Dad would want me to pay his respects, but I don't know where Mr. Langham would be staying, or whether he's been and gone. Do you think you could check it out with authorities on the qt and let me know? . . . All right then, thanks much."

He hung up and looked at me. "Don't panic. It'll be an unofficial off-the-record check for the Canadian government. Can't possibly get anyone in trouble, and at least we'll know whether the police were giving you the straight dope from immigration. He'll call back in a few hours. Meanwhile, what do you want to do? It will be much too late then to go back to Torremolinos tonight."

My eyes flared. "I have to! I can't stay in a hotel without a passport, and I *won't* stay with Uncle Tom. He'd keep me on a ball and chain till he put me on a New York plane."

"Stay here. Ascension will chaperone, in case you're worried about propriety or my intentions. *I'm* more worried about your safety. Tell me again what that man looked like who's been following you."

I repeated the description, focusing my memory as if it were a camera lens. "It's such a—a commonplace description," I finished. "There are hundreds of Spaniards around who look like that. Even the gold tooth."

"But you don't really think so," Quent finished quietly. "Too much coincidence. Too much, entirely." It was an echo of what I had thought myself.

The day was waning. Quent told Ascension that I was staying; that we would be dining in ("safer," he murmured to me in an aside). We went out to the walled patio, heady with the scent of oranges, and Quent took me around his mother's border gardens, pointing out the flowers. We had fruit punch, and presently, when the moon had risen, we had seafood paella and fruit flan.

We were just finishing when Ascension appeared to announce a telephone call. The man at the Canadian embassy confirmed what the police had said. There was no record of Gabriel Langham entering the country.

"Why are you shaking?" Quent said suddenly. He came over to put his arm around me. "*You* know he's in the country."

"If he is."

"You're not losing faith already, are you? There are a dozen reasons, and probably more ways, why he could have gotten in without record. Illegal, yes, but not immoral. I've read his books, and I can't believe he'd be involved in anything really wrong."

And then he stopped talking and just held me until my shaking ceased.

7

We returned to Torremolinos at the same time of day that I had first arrived. Siesta time. The same dim coolness of the lobby, the same man behind the desk, the same look of suspicion and dismissal. Only this time, Quent was with me.

Clearly, that only made the manager more suspicious. He shook his head curtly when I produced my father's picture. *Nada*, that man was not here, had never been here. When I asked for a registry card he shook his head. "You cannot stay here. We are all full."

Quent pinched me before I could say anything. "Then we will take the luggage you have stored for the young lady."

"The porter is not here. I cannot leave the desk to look."

"We'll get it ourselves." I could be as curt as he. I swept into the porter's den before he or Quent could protest, for an idea had popped into my brain. When Quent followed me in, I was working my way swiftly along the shelves.

"What are you—"

"Shut up," I hissed. "I'm looking for—Quent, that's *it!*"

It sat on the next-to-the-top shelf, half hidden behind a case of tennis racquets: a battered, nondescript American Tourister, the flight labels all removed. The handle tag read "Walter Brown, Toledo, Ohio." So the La Colomba management never *had* heard of Gabriel Langham!

"How can you be sure it's his bag?" Quent asked reasonably, scanning the tag.

"I must have packed that bag at least fifty times. I've traveled with it. That jagged scratch on the side came from the luggage chute in Rome, and there's a spot on the back where Callie and I spilled nail polish when we were kids."

I reached for the handle, and Quent jerked me away. Before I knew what was happening, he was stiff-arming me out of the porter's den. The manager did not look up, but I knew, with the clarity that anger brings, that he had been listening for our slightest word. Thank God we'd stuck to whispers, and *damn* Quent for making it impossible for me to speak up now! My arm was going to be black and blue.

"We've changed our minds. I'll come back for the bag after we've found the young lady a hotel room." Quent spoke in that maddeningly superior male tone and accompanied his words with a flash of his diplomatic passport. The manager was suddenly all charm. They concluded their exchange with a flurry of civilities.

I could only just contain my rage until we were outside. "What do you think you're—"

"As you told me, shut up." Quent hurried me along

the drive. But once out of sight of the hotel door, he abandoned the route to the bus depot and pulled me through the jungle plantings toward the condominium tower and into the elevator. A distinguished elderly couple shared it, so I seethed in silence until we were in what was presumably the Robards' apartment. Then Quent let go of me, and I swung on him.

"What's the big idea? That was my father's suitcase, and we could have gotten—"

"No, we couldn't. Do you think that half-baked caballero would have let you go one step with it?" Quent threw a closet open, began pulling out sports equipment. "If my sister just hasn't taken—Thank the Lord! It probably wasn't stylish enough for her anymore."

He yanked out a battered American Tourister case—the same gray, the same model.

Quent dumped it in front of me triumphantly. "Now, if we can just get the travel stickers soaked off, *voila!* The old switcheroo. What time did you say that manager goes to dinner?"

It took us the better part of the afternoon to get those labels off, and the process involved the bath brush, razor blades and his sister Ellen's nail polish remover. "Good thing she's not here," Quent commented, soaking off adhesive with the solvent. "She's insanely protective of her beauty aids."

"Where is your sister?"

"Spending a month with a school friend at their horse ranch. Paying more attention to friend's tall, handsome brother than to the horses. Not that she's bad, as sisters go," he added judiciously. "Just mad." He looked at me and grinned. "No way can I imagine her sitting on the edge of a bathtub with a guy, scrubbing a ratty old suitcase and getting soaked."

It dawned on me then just what I must look like.

Luckily, I was able to repair the damages before Quent's college friends from poolside returned. They were, it developed, also staying at the condo. By now all talk of finding a hotel room had been dropped. I was accepted uncritically as Quent's "bird," camping out there with all the rest. "In Ellen's bedroom," Quent said severely. "The rest of you clowns go back to the sleeping bags on the terrace."

What Callie wouldn't make of all this, I thought.

It would be some time yet before we could make the luggage switch. Meanwhile we sat on the terrace with the others, having snacks and fruit juice and trying to act as though nothing serious was on our minds. Finally, the college crowd departed in search of dinner, making ribald comments about our not joining them. Quent waited at the door until he heard the elevator bearing them rattle off.

"Better give it another fifteen minutes, in case someone's forgotten something and comes back." I watched the clock tick the time away, scarcely breathing. Then Quent picked up the suitcase and grinned crookedly.

"Wish me luck." He went away.

The condo seemed silent after he was gone. As the last twilight vanished I sat on the terrace, lamps unlit. At last I heard the click of the latch.

"Got it. And yours. I put the luggage tag on our substitute." Not stopping to flick on the lights, Quent strode directly to Ellen's bedroom, and I followed. He locked the door, pulled the draperies shut at the windows before turning on a lamp. We stared at the bag, so worn and so innocuous in the middle of the red and black woven Spanish spread.

"It's locked, of course," Quent said.

"Get me a fine screwdriver. Or some pointed scissors." It was Dad's one bad habit, the way he was forever losing luggage keys. How many times I'd heard him murmur, "Don't know why I bother anyway, it's so easy to break in," as he jimmied these very catches. I knew it *was* these very catches even before I snapped them open, saw the shabby trenchcoat and old brown sweater.

Quent reached over me for the sweater. "Labels carefully removed. And the same thing with the raincoat, see?" He was turning both of them inside and out, examining pockets, linings, seams. "Somebody didn't want anything identified. Either the owner, or—" He didn't finish. His face suddenly intent, he almost pushed me to one side. "Excuse me, a man can tell more things from another man's clothes than a woman can."

"They're *my father's* clothes!"

"Sarah, you can't know that." Quent stopped a moment, carefully patient. "These are perfectly ordinary, middle-aged traveling American's stuff. Nothing distinctive except that everything that *could* distinguish them has been removed."

"*I* can distinguish them! See that darn in the sweater elbow? I did that, because I've been at Dad for years to throw the old thing out and he won't do it. It reeks of his pipe tobacco."

"Other men wear out their elbows and smoke that brand." Quent pulled out some wadded-up laundry that was covering something bulky, and my throat constricted. *Bozo.*

"If you try that typewriter," I said shakily, "you'll find a chip out of the capital E. And the H key sticks." I turned away quickly so he could not see my stinging eyes.

There was a silence, then I heard a catch being snapped and the roller turned. Keys clicked. At last Quent said in an altered voice, "I'm sorry. Don't think I doubted your knowledge, but one needs proof."

I nodded tiredly and got out that dog-eared letter Dad had mailed me and, with Quent, made a close comparison. As I did, the sickness in me grew.

"Nothing would have made Dad voluntarily leave Bozo behind. The suitcase and the clothes, yes. I can imagine his removing labels if he wanted to throw people off his trail. But not his typewriter! It's—it's his extra arm. And he didn't *expect* to go away! He wrote me he'd be here!"

"A lot can happen in the time it takes a letter to go from Spain to the U.S." Quent dumped the last items from the suitcase onto the bed and sat down in a facing chair. "All right, let's say it straight. We're talking about possible kidnapping, possible government cover-up, a possible deliberate vanishing act—executed meticulously, but so suddenly the man didn't even have a chance to notify his daughter." He looked at me and frowned. "Odd if he should have engineered this with such precaution and yet run the risk of your doing exactly what you did— phone him under his right name."

"He thought I wouldn't," I said miserably. "He said not to, that *he'd* phone *me* . . . only then Selena got hurt. Oh, *why* didn't I wait like he told me to? First calling, and then coming here—and asking, both times, for Gabriel Langham. All I did was place him in more danger."

"I didn't mean that," Quent said quickly. "I just meant he must have had urgent reasons for not calling—or for leaving quickly."

"You'll never make me believe he was doing something wrong!"

"For Pete's sake!" Quent exploded. "We're not going to get anywhere if you're constantly trying to defend your father to me! Let's look at this logically. Your father was on the trail of a story. Big, front-page exposé! Something that he might or might not tell your embassy friend about, but that was serious enough to make him enter this country under a phony passport. Stop glaring at me, Sarah; there are all sorts of ways a person with your dad's background and connections could accomplish that. Now, what has he been really worked up about lately? He needn't have mentioned it as a book idea, some issue about which he felt strongly. Perhaps something that was in the news, something in which he thought the media or the governments concerned were haring off in the wrong direction."

"*They're on the wrong track . . . it's not that simple. . . .*" Dad's words shrieked back into my mind, and with them a picture of the two of us watching television together on a wintry Sunday evening. My mouth felt dry. "There is something . . . something I'd thought of, but I haven't mentioned because I didn't want to be put down one more time."

"For God's sake, tell me."

"There was a show on American TV last year. I think it was a rerun with an update. About one of our diplomatic attachés held hostage somewhere by a terrorist group."

"Which one?" Quent demanded.

"That's the point. The commentator said it was supposed to be *one*, but he wondered if it could be more than one. And suddenly Dad began to wonder if there was a whole linked-up network between the different groups: Bader-Meinhof, Red Brigade, PLO, Provisional IRA."

Quent whistled. "Your father was sure stirring up a hornets' nest if he decided to pursue that hunch."

"That's just it, that's what his agent said Dad told her." I searched my memory for an accurate quote. "He told her, this could be the most important book he'd ever write—that he'd gotten the idea from TV and now had a chance of getting proof if he acted quickly."

"And off he tore, without giving you any clue?"

"He said he didn't know *where* the trail would lead." I remembered something else. "He said he'd have to make another trip during the summer, that maybe then I could come along. He said to Germany or Italy. Or Ireland."

All countries identified with the terrorist groups I'd named. We just looked at each other. Quent asked, very matter-of-factly, "What was that TV commentator suggesting might be the link between the groups?"

"Arms smuggling. And fund-raising. He said all the terrorist groups needed money, and some of them might try to raise money together, that the groups might be extorting money under false pretenses from Americans who thought they were contributing to democracy-minded 'freedom groups' in oppressed regimes." My breath caught. "That's when Dad said it, about being on the wrong track and things not that simple."

"What did he mean?"

I frowned. "I think he meant the *need* for money wasn't the connecting link. He said the terrorist cells probably had more hot cash than they knew what to do with. And then he got this queer look on his face and said, 'I wonder . . .'"

The silence settled.

"That's it," Quent said at last, slowly. "Hot cash. Laundered money."

"What?"

"When people are buying arms illegally, money has to change hands in ways that can't be traced. Not by checks or currency numbers or bank deposits. If you're talking about donations to supposedly charitable organizations ending in the wrong hands, you're talking millions. Billions, maybe. And how does it get to the arms suppliers? A 'charitable organization' has to keep legitimate-appearing books. And people crossing international borders have to declare large sums of money, in whatever form. So it means covert transfers, probably in cash. It means innocuous couriers traveling on legitimate business." He stopped.

"Like an author on research?" I asked steadily. "Or someone traveling on a forged passport?"

"Have you never heard of infiltration?" Quent countered quietly. I suddenly felt cold. I started going through the heap of Dad's belongings—anything to keep my hands from shaking.

"You won't find anything," Quent said, watching.

Even the numbers of our local laundry had been removed. Someone had been very careful. I bent over the suitcase, doggedly removing everything. The only odd item was a Spanish newspaper, less than two weeks old, with a large corner torn off. I searched madly for the corner and didn't find it. At last I was down just to the molded shell, its lining laminated smoothly, its rims sharp metal—

Sharp.

I thrust a hand toward Quent without even looking. "Give me the scissors." He did so at once. With scissors and fingernails, I pried at the inner metal of the curved back corners.

"What?" Quent asked.

"There's a rough place . . . things slide up under and catch. Once part of a good skirt got left behind, and I was so mad—" I had the rim bent loose now, just a little. Quent vanished, returned with a flat slender knife. Cautiously, I slid the blade in, slid it around. . . .

When I withdrew it, a strip of paper followed.

Just a part of the missing corner. But it was stained with ballpoint ink that had bled through from the other side. Was it Quent who turned it over, or I? I don't remember, yet in a moment we were bent over it, heads together, staring at the fragmentary phrases.

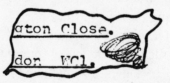

And the doodle, miscroscopic, a twisting funnel like the eye of a tornado. The writing might be too scant for identification, but I would know that doodle anywhere.

Dad had written this fragment of an address on a Spanish newspaper less than two weeks ago; Dad, who supposedly had not entered Spain.

"*Close*," Quent said tensely. "That's a British term. Like a dead-end street, or court . . . and *don WCl.* I'd gamble anything it's an address in London." He straightened, concentrating furiously. "Your father could have stumbled onto an address, scribbled it onto his newspaper for safekeeping. Then thrust it in the suitcase for safekeeping—"

"Or someone else did. Someone who didn't want it found. And a piece got caught when that someone pulled it out in a hurry and ripped off the corner," I stared at it hopelessly. "It's so little to go on. We can't even be sure it has anything to do with . . . And why *England?*"

"England," Quent said, "is close to Ireland. And terrorist bombings have not been unknown there lately." His matter-of-factness sent a chill up my spine. "Easily reached from the States, and from the Continent, yet removed from the center of covert action. You don't see armed guards in camouflage suits stationed in London airports, as you sometimes do in Rome. The British don't expect anything uncivilized to occur. Think, Sarah. Has anything to do with your father indicated a recent link to England?"

"He never even mentioned it. And he would have; he knows how I loved it in Lon—" I stopped, transfixed. "Quent, that letter. The one that was left for me at La Colomba, I thought something about it was familiar. Quent, the paper—"

I got it out, and we both looked at it — heavy, warm gray, its top slightly crooked as though a heading had been cut off. Not cheap, not easily come by, not something you'd expect a quick note to be written on—or a warning. "I've only seen paper like this one place before. At the Savoy Hotel in London. Theirs has a little pastel bouquet of flowers printed on top, with the name. I even took some back home with me, but I didn't tell Dad because I knew he'd tease me."

My head was starting to hurt. "It doesn't make sense," I said slowly. "Why a letter to me, here, on English paper? It wasn't *mailed*. There's no stamp and no address. I don't recognize the handwriting, but the writer had to know about Bad Penny." I had already told Quent the significance of the phrase. "What does it prove? And why are they trying to get rid of me?"

"It proves the international connection," Quent said flatly. "Someone's writing on English paper to threaten an American girl in Spain with danger to her father, who's interested in Ireland, Italy and Germany. And it proves *you're* dangerous in some way. Either you know something you're not aware of, or you're getting too close to something—or you're evidence of a connection between them and Gabriel Langham. That could be why your father vanished. Or was persuaded to."

The words hung in the air. Quent stood up, thrusting his hands into his pockets. "Enough of this for now. We can't do anything else tonight. I'll stash this stuff behind the junk in Ellen's closet, and we'd better go get some dinner somewhere. You're about her size. If you put on one of her outfits and tie a scarf around your head, we should be able to put one over on that creep who's been following you around."

Quent was right. In Ellen's wildly striped, oversized knit top and tight pants I didn't know myself. Especially once I'd added headscarf, floppy hat and dark glasses at Quent's insistence.

"After dark? It's crazy!" I protested. Quent chuckled.

"Ellen's crowd would think it's cool. They all go around looking like international film starlets in disguise. Not that Ellen needs disguising, but with the sunshades and all that hair I can scarcely see her face." The words were sardonic, but it was clear that he felt both amusement and affection for his sister.

The disguise worked. Neither in the taxi nor in the cafe where we ate and danced, nor on our return was there any sign of the man with the golden tooth.

Dinner was heavenly, in spite of—*because* of—our being unable to speak of the things that were uppermost in our minds. Instead we talked about our childhoods and our travels. We both loved London, we both were disappointed in Paris. Quent told me about student life at Oxford. I told him funny stories about me and Callie.

I didn't feel upset until we were back in the fortunately still-empty condo. Then all the panic, the sense of urgency and the need for action that had been in abeyance descended on me. I pulled off the disguising headgear and paced restlessly as Quent closed the blinds and turned on lights. A glimpse of myself in a tall mirror brought a giggle that verged on hysteria. "If Uncle Tom could see me now! He must have been half out of his skull when I didn't turn up at his house as ordered.

Serves him right, after the way he took Dad's disappearance in stride. As soon as I go back there, he'll slap me on a plane for home, but I've got to go back or I'll have no passport, and I have to get that passport or I can't do anything about following up on that address—Ooohhh!" I ran my fingers through my hair until it looked wild enough to go with Ellen's outfit. "What am I going to do?" I wailed.

I was really asking myself, not him. Quent looked surprised. "Do? Stay here, where Gold-tooth can't find you. I'll stock the fridge and the cupboards, so you needn't worry."

"And where will you be?" I asked involuntarily.

Quent looked even more astonished. "In London, of course. I'll catch the morning flight, and I won't come back till I've enlisted our embassy there and Scotland Yard and checked out every *gton Close* in WC1 and elsewhere."

"Do you seriously expect me to sit here in hiding while *you* go chasing around looking for *my father?*"

"My dear girl, aren't you forgetting, you don't have a passport?"

If that kindly patronizing manner was what he'd learned at Oxford, I never wanted to see the place again. "Aren't you forgetting," I said distinctly, "that you told me there were a dozen ways for somebody with diplomatic connections to get in and out of countries without a legal passport? Did you mean that, or were you just trying to 'make the poor girl feel better'—or put down my father?"

Quent was clearly jolted. "You're not suggesting trying to get yourself into England on a forged passport or false identity!"

"I don't give two hoots if it's forged or false or borrowed! It's *my* father who's missing, *my* father who's in danger, and for that matter maybe I am too, and I'm *not* going to hide out here and water the geraniums while you go charging off pretending to be James Bond!"

"All right, all right! I didn't mean to start the American Revolution over again. I only thought—"

"Think again," I interrupted dangerously.

"I'm thinking, I'm thinking. If only Dad were in this country—although maybe under the circumstances it's a good thing he's not. I don't think we can stretch diplomatic immunity to someone who's not a member of the family." Quent broke off. He looked me over, deliberately, from top to bottom and then back up again, and a slow smile spread across his face.

My face crimsoned, and I strove for dignity, all too conscious of how I looked in Ellen's crazy clothes. "Well? Does your Oxford expertise extend to the Torremolinos blackmarket in purloined passports?"

"Not purloined. Borrowed. Thanks to your slightly overheated verbiage, I have had an absolutely brilliant inspiration. Sarah Langham isn't going to go to England." He held up his hand at my screech of outrage and went on. "Sarah Langham has vanished into seclusion, visiting friends of ours in the horse country. You can send your Uncle Tom a card to that effect. The ranch, believe it or not, has its own armed guards, so if Goldtooth intercepts the post card, he'll get what he deserves. Meanwhile, you'll be in London. Not as Sarah Langham. As my sister Ellen."

8

"Fasten your seat belts, please." The flight attendant's voice came over the loudspeakers as I clutched the unfamiliar handbag and felt the clamminess of fear well over me. It was like a reliving of my arrival in Spain, with one great difference. Quent was beside me.

Two great differences. In the tooled leather pouch I gripped was Ellen's passport. My feet, red-nailed, were thrust into Ellen's high-heeled wooden clogs; I wore Ellen's designer jeans and embroidered Spanish blouse. My eyes behind Ellen's dark glasses wore more make-up than I'd ever tried. My hair was curled with Ellen's curling-iron into a wild dark tangle, and the front locks, cut to cheekbone-length and bleached, hid my forehead behind a tousled flip. Quent had cut those locks, working from his sister's photo. Together, he and I had bleached them with stuff we found in the medicine closet of Ellen's bathroom.

In Ellen's clothes I had flown to Madrid with Quent that morning. We had slipped into the Robards' house, choosing a time when Ascension always went to Mass. There, Quent had hunted up Ellen's passport and his own. He had packed one of Ellen's suitcases with Ellen's clothes. I had added the contents of my own suitcase, brought from Torremolinos in Quent's own bag while mine stayed hidden in the back of that condo closet. I was leaving no clues to myself behind me, and besides, I might need to look like Sarah, and not Ellen, once I was in London.

Quent had also telephoned Jerez while I sat listening, tense and silent. "El? Me. You're staying there a couple more weeks, aren't you? Look, I need to borrow some of your things. And I need you out of public circulation while I'm using them, so lie low, will you? No getting your name or picture in the papers for anything, OK?" His tone had altered. "I can't explain, but it's an emergency. Good thing your school's on vacation, too. I wish Dad were here. Thanks, El. You're a good kid."

And so the real Ellen Robards was deep in Jerez with her Spanish friend and her friend's horses and her friend's brother. And here was I, circling into Heathrow Airport with borrowed identification and a bad case of nerves.

Act cool, because Ellen always acted cool, even when she wasn't. Remember to respond when Quent called me Ellen. Remember he was supposed to be my brother. Be careful not to break my neck on the ramp in these high heels. Now we are safely into the airport, heading toward Immigration. Remember I was carrying a Commonwealth passport.

My customs and immigration cards were all filled out, from information provided in the passport. Don't act nervous. Quent was propelling me ahead of him in line, so that must be where Ellen would have stood. What do

I say to the immigration man? How do I sound Canadian? Not that Quent had much of an accent, but he phrased some things differently.

To my relief, as we reached the counter, Quent took the cards and passport from me and handed them over with his own. Did the dark glasses scream disguise? No, other people too were wearing them. The young inspector took a quick look at the diplomatic passport, smiled at me pleasantly.

"Will you be visiting in England long, Miss Robards?"

"About a week." It was Quent who answered. "I'm going to show her my House at Oxford. We'll be staying with friends."

"You're not sure where, yet, I see." The inspector was looking at the forms where the Oxford address was given as our place of visit.

Quent grinned. "No, sir. Wherever we get the best invitation! But mail sent care of the University will always reach me. Or through our Embassy."

Reminded of our diplomatic status, the inspector smiled again and nodded. "Have an enjoyable visit, Miss Robards, Mr. Robards."

We were through.

My legs felt weak, but Quent didn't give me a chance to humor them. He rushed me onto the moving walkway to the luggage carousels.

More quickly then I believed possible, the bags came through, and we headed towards the Customs aisle marked "Nothing to Declare."

We emerged into the chaos of Heathrow at rush hour.

"The Underground, I think," Quent decided, picking up the bags and plunging toward it. I hurried to keep up.

I had no English money, but Quent did, and he bought tickets. We squeezed into two of the few remaining seats as the door slammed shut.

"Quent? Where are we going?" I had to shout above the subway's roar.

"School of Economics. It rents out dorm rooms during the holidays. I have a friend who goes there."

Get out at Piccadilly; change platforms, board train for Goodge Street. When we emerged, the sky was nearly dark. Quent looked at me and laughed. "Aren't you going to take those dark glasses off?" I did so, blinking.

I felt naked without them, as though the falseness of my painted face was showing, but no one that we passed looked at me oddly. We hurried along the quiet streets and turned in the door of Carr-Saunders Hall.

Quent took care of registering, producing our passports and his own Oxford University ID. The young graduate student manning the desk produced two room keys. "Loo and bath room down the hall. Cafeteria upstairs closes in half an hour, and we lock the front door for the night at midnight. After that, you'll have to ring—try not to! You're welcome to watch the telly in the lounge, if you would like."

The rooms were institutional, high and tiny. Mine held a bed, a straight chair, small desk and a narrow closet half-lined with shelves. I was looking at it despairingly when Quent appeared in my doorway chuckling.

"Not quite the Savoy, is it? Sorry, I forgot."

"Quent, when can we—"

"Not tonight." Quent's eyes flicked warningly toward the wall, and I grasped that it was paper-thin. "Let's go out and get some dinner. Anything you want to bring along?"

"I have everything." Only the clothes were in Ellen's suitcase; our notes, Dad's letter and the warning note were in my purse. I slung the long strap diagonally across my shoulder and clutched the bag between my arm and my left side. There would be no third robbery.

London at night, with Quent, was not the London I had visited with Dad. We took a bus toward Piccadilly and headed for a pub—below ground level, crowded, noisy, filled with smoke and students. "Grab a table," Quent ordered, heading for the buffet bar. Presently he reappeared, balancing plates of shepherd's pie on top of mugs of cider.

Across the room, of all things, somebody was playing honky-tonk piano. Close by us a video game emitted shrill bleeps. "Ever been here before?" Quent asked.

I shook my head. "It's—interesting."

Quent laughed. "It's also safe. You never meet anyone here you ever saw before—"

"Quentin! You sly fox, when did you get back in town?" Somebody tall and male was bearing down on us, and I didn't need to be told he was the Oxford version of the college jock.

"Hello, George," Quent said without enthusiasm. George took that for an invitation and pulled up a stool.

"Well, hello there! Where has old Robards been hiding you?" George turned what he considered his charm full on me, and my skin crawled. Then it prickled with another emotion as he said, "Say, Quent, when are you going to bring that gorgeous sister of yours back up here? Not that you need her company with a doll like this around, but you might consider the rest of us poor lonely souls."

My hand jerked, causing cider to slosh onto the table. Quent remained calm. "Ellen's here. She just has no time to waste on you this trip. Sally, this is George. Note that I'm not supplying last names, addresses or references, so if you feel like taking that as a hint, old buddy—"

"All right, all right, I get the message." George winked at me and blundered away, to have better luck with a girl across the room.

I let my breath out shakily. "Quent—"

"I know. Relax. We'll talk about it later. Eat your shepherd's pie, it's pretty good."

It was not till we were back in Carr-Saunders that we were able to talk. Quent followed me into my room, shut and locked the door, and to my surprise took a transistor radio from his pocket. He flicked it on, loud.

"There, that's the best conversation-muffling device I can imagine. Let's make plans, before somebody starts pounding on the wall."

"Quent, I'm getting scared. That friend of yours—"

Quent grimaced. "No friend. He's a pest who came on too strong to Ellen and got what he deserved. Which proves my sister has some sense, after all."

"He knew I wasn't her."

"And that's *all* he knows," Quent said firmly. He did not add what I had already realized. We now had a new, unanticipated danger—of having my cover blown when I was masquerading somewhere as Ellen. I hadn't known she had been with him in England. "All right," Quent went on as though he'd read my mind, "we'll have to split up part of the time tomorrow. I'll go to our embassy without you."

"I'll try the Savoy. Everybody there knows Dad. And I'll talk to his agent and his British publishers."

"And Scotland Yard."

"Not yet. If he's been kidnapped, that could put him in greater danger." But that was not the only reason I sheered off involving the police, and Quent knew it, damn him.

"I thought you weren't giving up faith in your father," he said pointedly.

"I'm not! I just don't think it would help right now to bring the authorities in. Help me get organized. We need a list of the evidence we have and the conjectures we make from it and our reasons for them."

Before a shout demanded that we "Turn that damn radio down," we had compiled not just that list, but another one of Dad's London haunts and contacts.

I went to sleep at last on the hard bed, staring out the window and wondering what Dad was seeing. The next thing I knew, there was knocking on my door and Quent's voice was calling, "Come on, Ellen! Let's get upstairs before they run out of eggs and bacon!"

He knew his dormitory cafeterias well. There were still eggs, but they were watery, and the bacon was half raw. After the meal, we went our separate ways: Quent to the embassy, I to the nearest bus stop in my borrowed clothes. With borrowed British money, too. We had concluded I'd better not try to change American money at a British bank with a Canadian passport. Quent had emptied his own wallet for me and gone off with one of my fifty-dollar bills, promising to get it changed himself. I had never gone around London on my own, and I dared not trust my knowledge on the subway. Oh, face it, I was afraid! It did no good to tell myself, as I did repeatedly, that I was in London, I was safe, there was no man with a gold tooth following me here. Besides, there was no reason for anyone to follow Ellen Robards!

The only catch was, I could not remain here long. It was Sarah Langham who would have to ask questions at the Savoy.

The Savoy was in east central London, but I headed west, past Piccadilly Circus, past Hyde Park to Harrods', London's fabulous department store. I took the escalator up to the service floor with its bank and travel office, its restaurants, its "Way In" coffee shop with disco music blaring. Ellen Robards went into the ladies' lounge, but it was Sarah Langham who came out of one of the private dressing cubicles that I had remembered. Ellen's jeans and top and heels were in my bag in place of the flats and shirt and denim skirt that I now wore. My hair was brushed straight again, and a wide scarf covered the bleached front section. The eye makeup was scrubbed off. I felt myself again; I also felt exposed.

"It's crazy," I told myself. "I'm safe here." No one had seen me slip into the last dressing room at the far end, and it would not have mattered if they had. The disguise had been only a means of getting me into the country without a passport, after all!

I even dared the subway for the trip to the Savoy. When I reached there, I almost laughed, everything was so *normal*. The same shabby, busy Strand with its businesses, theaters and tourists. The same lovable London cabs, stolid and reassuring, nudging among the Rolls Royces into the Savoy's drive; the same elderly doorman in his vaguely Edwardian uniform; the same wood-paneled lobby with its aura of rectitude and money.

I went to the hall porter's desk, the memory of Dad's voice sharp in my ears. "The English hall porter is an intitution, a cross between Santa Claus and a nanny. When I was young, some of them even kept me going between paychecks. They never forget a face." This one had not forgotten mine.

"Miss Langham! We haven't had the pleasure of serving you in three years." For a moment I thought he was going to add, *how the child has grown.* "Will you be staying here for a holiday?"

"No—I'm with friends." I forced my voice to remain casual. "Have you seen my father? I want to surprise him, and I—understood he might be here."

The dignified face above the uniform was regretful. "He hasn't been here since—I believe it was last October."

"Are you *sure?*"

Faint aloofness, faint reproach: "Miss Langham, I can assure you if Mr. Langham had been here, I would have known."

"If he comes in, if he's alone—only if he's alone—tell him I'm looking for him. Don't tell anyone else." I improvised a reason. "It's a surprise."

A nod of assent. Out into the Strand again. Why hadn't I asked the porter for a London map? I forced myself to visualize the city's layout. West toward Charing Cross and Trafalgar Square, then up behind St. Martin's-in-the-Fields—that was the way to Dad's London agent, whom Miss McCausland had suggested that I contact. There was a unisex hairdresser on one side and a Greek-Italian cafe serving morning coffees on the other. I glanced towards it; froze; then relaxed. The man beyond the window glass was of Gold-tooth's build. But this man wore British clothes and was surely older.

I went into the agency building's tiny lobby, pushed the button on the brass elevator cage. The car was interminably slow in coming, even slower in crawling up to the fourth floor. Then a locked door and an old-fashioned doorbell to be twisted and another wait before an elderly receptionist appeared. At last I was inside Mr. Griffin's office, and Mr. Griffin—tall, bent, fragile as old paper—was pressing biscuits and milky coffee on me. How delightful of me to stop by; how regrettable that he could not give me any news about my father. He had seen or heard nothing since that pleasant visit last October.

"Mr. Griffin, can you tell me what my father was working on?"

He shook his head, smiling faintly. "Gabriel does like to tease, you know. He hinted it was something enormously important—he always does feel that, doesn't he? And he's so often right."

I wanted to scream, to shatter the ancient placidity of the place. I said tightly, "I think he's investigating terrorist activity. I think he's in grave danger."

"Dear me," Mr. Griffin said mildly. He didn't bat an eye. It occurred to me he must have lived through many bombs in the London blitz. His face looked, if possible, even more like an old marble effigy. "That is distressing. But I shouldn't alarm yourself too much, Miss Langham. Gabriel has a cat's instincts for survival. And for capitalizing on a dangerous situation. You know what he says, the bad penny always turns up, hmm?"

There was that phrase again.

Mr. Griffin telephoned Dad's London publisher. He, too, knew nothing. I made my way at last back into William IV Street, uneasy and discouraged.

It was midday now, and office workers were hurrying to lunch. The cafe next door was jammed. Where now? I wondered, heading mechanically toward Trafalgar Square. Maybe I should buy a sandwich to take out and eat by the fountains. But when I had finally waited my turn for "a plowman's"—sharp Cheddar cheese and lettuce, with chutney and a slab of crusty bread—I found a seat empty near the pub door and sank into it gratefully.

The two typically British businessmen across from me left soon after. Their place was taken by another man who was typical London in a very different way. His short, stocky figure was encased in trousers of a brightish green and the brashest black and white checked sports jacket I had ever seen. I glanced toward him, started to look away, caught sight of his head and gazed, fascinated. Shoe-button black eyes matched very short-cropped black hair, topped by one of those very narrow-brimmed bowler hats. From below his cheekbones, his face bulged into fleshy jowls, so that he looked for all the world as if the top half and bottom half of his head had been mismatched. Like something out of Dickens. Or out of one of Dad's own Cockney-racetrack-tout tall stories. I wished sharply that Dad was there beside me.

A girl sat down opposite me, pretty in a short-skirted bright blue dress. We nodded and half-smiled, the way you do with strangers when you share a table. Then she looked at me closely. "Don't I know you?"

"I don't think—"

"Of course, I do. Never forget a face, that's me. D'you work in publishing? I'm Marla Finch, old Lattimore's secretary, at Esterley and James." She snapped her fingers. "You're What'shisname's daughter—can't think of it now, but he writes those behind-the-scenes-top-secrets books!" She smiled brightly. "I met you when you both came to the office a few years ago. You were just a kid then, of course. Probably wouldn't have remembered you, except that the Griffin just telephoned Mr. Lattimore, asking about your dad. I say, is he doing a new one?"

"Not that I know of." I cut in to stop her chatter, glancing nervously around. No one was looking at us. The man in the checked jacket was reading a racing form. Esterley and James *was* Dad's publisher. I lowered my voice. "That was me calling—at least, Mr. Griffin was trying to locate my father for me." I was being so careful not to mention his name. Could I keep her from doing so? My mind raced. "I think he's in England. You're right, he *is*—working on something special, but we mustn't let anyone know."

"Gotcha." She winked, grinning broadly. "Lattimore won't be half pleased when he hears about it. Funny, him not knowing." Her smile faded, and she frowned slightly. "I heard what he said on the telephone, about not seeing your guv since last year. Thing is, I could have sworn I saw him myself, a day or so ago. But it wouldn't have done to contradict the big boss, would it?"

I leaned forward tensely. "Marla, where did you see him? I have to get in touch with him—it's important."

She concentrated. "Up by the British Museum some-where, I think. My boyfriend gets ever so cultural on the weekends, can you imagine? And I can't be sure it was your dad really, can I? Don't have a photo in your wallet, do you?" I produced it, but after a moment she shook her head. "Could be, but I couldn't swear. Tell you what, love, give me your number, and if I catch a glimpse of him again I'll let you know."

"You can reach me through a friend." I scribbled the Robards' name and the Carr-Saunders address on a paper napkin and passed it over. Marla thrust it in her bag and drained her mug.

"Ta for now. If I don't get back to Esterley and James I'll lose my pay packet. Keep smiling, love."

Keep smiling. It was easier said than done. Yet someone had seen Dad, I reminded myself fiercely; some-one had seen him in public. My mind blotted out Marla's hesitation, wrestled with the oddity of Dad's not having contacted either Mr. Lattimore or Mr. Griffin. Even if he were under cover, even if he weren't ready to reveal his story—it was not like him. It was even less like him than traveling around Europe on a false passport.

Or *was* he in England on a false passport?

I left my bread and cheese half-eaten, my cider half-drunk. I went out into Charing Cross, swept along in a crush of others exiting the pub. A cab swept up and I dove for it, saying firmly, "The United States Embassy."

9

The U.S. Embassy filled a city block, looking out on Grosvenor Square. A long line of people was waiting to apply for visas as I went up the broad stone steps, and high above the row on row of blank windows, a carving of an American eagle spread its wings. It was all handsomely modern and institutional, and it gave me a chill.

Inside the glass doors, before a bare wood wall, an elderly porter stood guard over a radar screen. It must have taken fifteen minutes and two phone calls before I was allowed inside.

"Through that door, up the stairs and to the counter where you see Marines. Someone will come down to meet you."

Inside were more lines, more waiting. At last a middle-aged man in a brown business suit came from the elevators, holding out his hand. "Miss Langham? I'm Ed Anderson. So you're Gabe Langham's daughter."

I was escorted upstairs, through what seemed miles of corridors hung with paintings and etchings of American Indian scenes. An American secretary, to whom I was introduced, smiled and said something complimentary about Dad's books. And in a large, light-filled office with comfortable chairs, I was given the same meaningless doubletalk Uncle Tom had handed me in Madrid.

"Now, Miss Langham, I wouldn't get alarmed. I know it's frightening for a young girl to not be able to reach her parent when she wants to—"

"It's not that at all!"

"—but you have to understand the way American businessmen zip around these days."

"Gabriel Langham's not a businessman. He's an investigative writer who gets right to the heart of dangerous situations."

"And does a good job of it, too, I might add. So I'm sure wherever he is, you needn't worry about his safety."

"Not even if he's mixed up with international terrorists and arms and money smuggling?"

"Now we don't know that he's looking into that, do we? We don't even know he's come to the U.K. In fact, Miss Langham, your imagination's been jumping to conclusions."

"My common sense and my knowledge of my father both tell me it's very likely that he came here. Willingly, or otherwise. So does the evidence."

"Ah, yes, the evidence." He glanced at the little pile, a benign smile on his face. "That scrap of address could have gotten caught in the suitcase any time. You did say your dad was over here last October." Mr. Anderson ignored completely the fragment of date printed on the paper. "Certainly, no matter how attached a writer may be to his typewriter, he doesn't cart it with him everywhere. And the Savoy's surely not the only place that uses that particular variety of paper."

"Can you honestly tell me there's no possibility of an international terrorist group laundering money here in London?"

"Certainly I can't tell you that. It would hardly fall in our department, would it? And Scotland Yard and the Special Branch don't file reports with us just because we're allies." Mr. Anderson chuckled. "Between you and me, I don't think they'd like our butting in. But I can tell you one thing." His face grew serious. "The U.S. Government does not, repeat *not*, use civilians to assist in any way in covert operations."

"What," I asked dangerously, "is the U.S. Government's position on civilian citizens being threatened or detained by terrorist groups?"

"But we really have no evidence of that being the case, do we? Only speculation. In any event, it would be Scotland Yard's show. That is, if the incident happened here. Actually, you've suggested it happened in Spain. Why didn't you report it to our Spanish colleagues?"

"I did," I said through gritted teeth. "They didn't believe it, either."

"There, you see?" Mr. Anderson spread his hands and smiled. "If I were you, I'd go back home and get on with all that school work and gymnastics competition." I had had to tell him that in the course of explaining Dad's reasons for refusing to take me with him. "I wouldn't be surprised if you found a letter from your dad waiting when you get there. Why, he may even have gone home himself already."

It was a possibility I hadn't thought of. A very, very slim possibility. I ought to call home just in case there'd been word, I thought, watching Mr. Anderson buzz his secretary.

"Miss Kirk, just check with U.K. Immigration and see if they have any record of Gabriel Langham coming into the country in the past month, will you?"

They didn't, of course. I got out of there before it occurred to Mr. Anderson to make inquiries about my own passport.

The sky had clouded while I was inside. Miss Kirk escorted me to a side exit door, and I went out into grayness and a raw wind that hinted rain. Where now, I wondered bleakly. The streets were all but deserted, and the spring flowers blew disconsolately in Grosvenor Square. I sat down on a park bench, staring at the statue of President Franklin Roosevelt, remembering his famous saying about there being "nothing to fear but fear itself." That was what *he* thought. All at once, I felt uneasy about being out in the open, about being alone. The windows on the serene façades around the square were like hundreds of staring eyes.

I should call home. From where? I would have no privacy at Carr-Saunders. There were public pay phones for international calls in Leicester Square. Thank goodness Quent had stuffed two twenty-pound notes in my hand that morning. I changed one note into coins by stopping in a luncheonette for a cup of tea. It was black and bitter, but it gave me enough strength to carry me to Leicester Square and make me ignore that continuing, unreasonable sensation that I was being watched.

In Leicester Square, among the pigeons and the skinheads and the punks with their Apache scalp-locks dyed neon colors, I dialed the long string of numbers that would reach Callie's home.

Callie was almost hysterical when she heard my voice. "Where are you? We tried to reach you at that hotel your dad wrote from, but they acted as if they'd never heard of you, and we've been worried sick!"

Thank heaven for Callie, who knew me so well I hadn't even had to give my name, who never made it necessary for me to finish sentences. "I'm in London," I said. "Can't explain now. Have you heard anything?"

"From your dad? No. Not directly. I remembered what his letter said about phoning you on Sunday night, so Mom and I went over to your house, just in case. There *was* an overseas call, but it was for you person-to-person, and when I tried to tell the operator I'd take it for you, the party on the other end hung up."

"Where were they calling from?"

"The operator wouldn't say. I'm sorry, Sar—"

"Callie!" I cut in desperately as the phone beeped that time was running out. "Has there been mail?"

"Just bills, and two college catalogues for you. Nothing pers—"

Beep-beep-beep-beep . . . The connection was broken, and I was out of coins. I put the receiver down, my mind swirling. *Go home and await instructions*, that warning note had said. Why had there been none? Because the writer knew I had not obeyed? Because it was all a macabre joke? Or worse?

I crossed Leicester Square, ignoring the skinheads who muttered comments on my anatomy as they looked me up and down. One of the movie theaters was showing an old James Bond movie. *In Her Majesty's Secret Ser-*

vice. Secret Service. Scotland Yard. They were the ones who handled terrorist activities. They were the ones who handled missing person cases. The movie stills on the front of the marquee made me suddenly, sickeningly aware of the dangers inherent in both those things.

I went down the stairs into the Leicester Square Underground Station, pushed coins into a ticket machine, scanned the multi-colored route map, my heart thumping. Fear of gettting lost no longer mattered nearly so much as getting to Scotland Yard as quickly as possible. Thank goodness the London Transit Authority posted maps of London on the station walls. I went down to the Northern Line platform, standing as far back from the edge as possible, feeling sick from the soot and closeness and distant engine roar. The train pulled in, and I boarded. Trafalgar Square; change to the District Line . . . Westminster . . . St. James Park . . . the stations and the people went by me like flashes in a kaleidoscope. I came out into stinging rain.

Not far away New Scotland Yard loomed like a glass eggcrate not yet finished. Bobbies in their distinctive helmets stood at the entrance. Inside was claustrophobic warmth and officialdom and the same noncommittal runaround. What it all boiled down to was that free adults had the right to vanish any time and anywhere they chose. Unless I had proof of a crime being committed, Scotland Yard could not step in.

What it boiled down to was that in the eyes of the Establishment—*every* Establishment—I was (a) wet behind the ears, (b) overimaginative, (c) acting like a hysterical female, and (d) I ought to be home like a good little girl. Nobody seemed to give a damn about linkages between terrorist groups and American money. Or about Dad.

The rain slapped at me as I emerged. My hair was soaked, losing the last remnants of its Ellen-flip. The subway entrance yawned, and it filled me with an unreasoning panic. I bent my head against the wet and plunged off towards Westminster, where I knew the bus lines stopped.

Rush hour traffic was starting now. If I wanted to head northwest towards Carr-Saunders I would have to catch a bus on the far side of Parliament Square. I crossed the first lane of traffic in the square to the narrow island and waited, with a crush of homebound commuters, for a red light to signal the second lane to stop.

I was on the edge of the island, peering through the rain to see if the bus was coming, when something struck me sharply in the shoulder. For a second I teetered, flailing for my balance. Then something—someone—shoved me, and I was going down. Down from the curb, into the path of an oncoming bus.

I think I screamed. I know I saw the red two-decker vehicle looming over me. But hands were catching me, jerking me sharply back.

I was on the island again then, my arms bruised and aching from their rough usage, my ankle throbbing from the twist I had given it as I fell. But I was alive. I was alive, and a small flock of worried Londoners were clucking over me.

I hope I was grateful. I'm afraid I sounded curt. I didn't even know who it was who'd saved me. I knew I didn't want to go to the hospital or the police or have "a nice cuppa tea" as my anxious audience suggested. All I wanted was to get home, and when for a wonder a taxi splashed to a stop to discharge a passenger, I dove inside it. I gave the address of Carr-Saunders hall and fell back against the black leather seat cushions, shaking.

I was still shaking when we reached the dormitory. Quent was waiting in the lobby, concern and anger mingled on his face.

"Where have you been? I though you were coming back in time for tea. Why didn't you phone?"

"Not here. Walk me upstairs."

Quent took a look at my face and did.

I climbed slowly, for my ankle was beginning to scream. He didn't see; he was ahead of me in his impatience. He'd collected the key to my room and had the door open before I reached it. I limped in, and Quent, turning back after he'd closed the door behind me, finally noticed. "What happened to your foot?"

"Somebody tried to kill me," I said flatly.

10

For once I'd jolted him. "What do you mean, somebody tried to kill you?"

"Just what I said. Somebody shoved me in front of a bus in Parliament Square."

Quent, baffled, anxious, seized on the one item that made sense. "What the hell were you doing in Parliament Square?"

"Trying to come back here from Scotland Yard. I know I wasn't going to go there, but it was the last thing left that I could think of." To my shame, I felt tears gathering in my eyes. "Look, if you're going to give me the third degree, do you mind if I sit down? I've had about all that I can take."

Quent snapped his transistor on, and a flood of BBC pop music poured out as he knelt to slip the shoe from my swelling foot. "Just a sprain, I think. Thank the Lord you weren't wearing Ellen's heels. What happened, and what makes you think somebody pushed you?"

"I know a poke in the shoulder when I feel it! If people hadn't grabbed me—" For a moment, horror washed over me. Quent cleared his throat, rooted in my bag for tissues and pressed them in my hand.

"You must have been standing too close to the edge," he said at last. My temper flared.

"Where else is there to stand at rush hour? And don't you dare tell me I'm imagining things! I was *pushed*."

"Why?" Quent asked reasonably. I just looked at him. "There's no reason for it," he went on in that logical tone. "If we were in Spain—but we're in England, and nobody knows you're you."

"Are you forgetting that I've been on Dad's trail all day? The Savoy, the agency, the embassy. *And* Scotland Yard."

"It's not likely your embassy or the Yard would want to bump you off. Or your dad's agent. And you haven't told anyone else who you are, have you?"

"Of course not." I stopped, and Quent caught me.

"What?"

"There was a girl in a pub—Dad's publisher's secretary—and she recognized me." I saw Quent about to explode, so I rushed on quickly. "I asked her if she'd seen Dad lately, and she thought she had. But we never spoke my name aloud, or his. She looked at his picture, but she couldn't be sure, so I gave her Ellen's name and this address and told her she could get in touch with me through her."

"For Pete's sake, Sarah! I know Americans are naïve, but do you have to be an utter fool? How do *you* know she was the publisher's secretary?"

"She said so . . ." My voice trailed off.

"If she'd told you she was Princess Diana's sister, would you have believed that, too? After what's happened already, you talk about your father in a public place, you show his picture and say you're looking for him! Yes, I know you didn't mention his name, but do you think any of the crowd your dad's mixed up in wouldn't have recognized the snapshot? And to cap it off you tie him to *Ellen Robards*, here."

"Nobody heard anything," I said with dignity. "Nobody could, except the man at the table with us, and he was wrapped up in the racing form."

"In public places, the walls have ears! Didn't you learn that much in Spain?" Quent grabbed me by the shoulders so hard I winced. "Don't tell *anyone anything*, do you hear me? And don't trust anyone. Not without proof. Even passports can be forged, remember?" He released me and stepped back, looking shaken. "Get cleaned up, and let's go out for dinner. And don't do anything like that again."

When Quent left, I took my wet clothes off, pulled on Ellen's robe and went down the corridor to the women's washroom. The hot shower enveloped me in a comforting cloud of steam, but there was little comfort for my mind. In front of the mirror afterwards, I combed my hair, feeling the ache in my shoulders as I raised my arms. On an impulse, I dropped the robe down and surveyed my body in the mirror. There were bruises on my arms where rescuers had grabbed me, bruises on my shoulders where Quent had done so later. There was also a circular bruise, turning purple, below my right shoulder blade.

So much for Quent's saying I'd imagined somebody pushing me.

Quent was right, though: who in England would

want to kill me? *Anyone to whom my following Dad is a threat,* my mind retorted. And reason countered, *Anyone who knew about it.* Not the police. Not Scotland Yard. Not Dad's agent or publisher; the thought of them mixed up in covert activities was too farfetched.

Who else knew?

The hall porter at the Savoy. The girl in the pub. Anyone else who overheard—except that our conversation would have meant nothing unless they had already been following me. And Quent.

My ears were ringing suddenly, and I felt a peculiar burning in my throat. Over the ringing was the memory of Quent's voice. *"Don't trust anyone. Not without proof."*

How did I know, really, that he was Quent Robards?

Because he'd told me so, and that was all.

It was crazy, it was paranoid, yet I could not flee from the doubt and panic that swept over me. I'd seen Quent's diplomatic passport. Passports could be forged. Or borrowed—I knew that, didn't I? I'd been in an apartment and a house that he'd said belonged to his family. Even that could have been arranged. His appearing twice, in the nick of time, to rescue me from being followed, could also have been arranged so I would trust him.

And I had trusted him. Why? Because he'd believed my story. Because he'd been sympathetic and helpful. Because something in me responded when he touched me, a corner of my mind added sickly. I didn't *know* he was connected with the Canadian embassy. I'd only heard him talk to what he said was the embassy on the telephone. Yet impulsively, without checking his credentials in the slightest, I'd told him all I knew about Dad's work. I'd put myself into his hands and followed him, on a borrowed passport, from Spain to Engand. It was one more example of my acting on the basis of Langham intuition, without the balance-force of Langham caution.

For a minute I clung to the edge of the wash basin as blackness and nausea swept me. Then reason returned, fighting back my panic inch by inch. All I have to do, I told myself carefully, is walk out of here to a telephone and call Mr. Anderson and tell him the whole story. He'll check with Uncle Tom and get me a passport and look after me till I'm safely on a plane for home.

I left the washroom, but I didn't go to the telephone. I went back to my cubicle, put on Ellen's plain black jersey dress and went downstairs to meet Quent for dinner.

He had dressed up in a suit and tie. "I thought we'd go out for a decent dinner." He ushered me out into Fitzroy Street and flagged a cab. "Better with your ankle," he murmured. I said nothing.

The cab delivered us to a restaurant near Leicester Square. I said little as we were seated at a banquette in red-and-gold Chez Solange and served peasant onion soup with a thick crust of cheese. Quent, seeing that I paid little attention to the menu, had ordered for me. "I almost always come here my first night in town. Been doing it ever since Dad and Mom brought us here as kids." It was a good thing, then, that I hadn't tried to pass myself off tonight as Ellen. The hairdo and makeup hadn't seemed worth the effort.

The soup was followed by a marvelous *coq au vin*. I had all I could do to pick at it. Quent noticed, finally.

"What's the matter?"

"I'm just not hungry."

"Ankle hurt?"

"All of me hurts." I reached for my water glass, and Quent's eyes fell on my bruised arm and his face altered.

"I'm sorry about that."

"Are you?"

"Ellen—"

"*Not now.*" It was all I could do to keep from shouting, *Don't call me that.* Quent looked at me oddly, but let it drop.

He ordered the house specialty for dessert, a banana-split confection with cassis syrup and fresh raspberries. It made me think of when I was in grade school and got three A's on my report card, and Dad would take me to the ice cream store to celebrate. My eyes blurred, and I could not swallow.

The rain had stopped, but the streets were like dark, wet mirrors when we emerged. The reflections of the neon signs shimmered, red and blue.

What was I going to do? I didn't know.

We got into a taxi and spun back to Carr-Saunders Hall. It was still early. Students were sprawled in front of the television set in the front lounge. Quent took hold of my arm—gingerly, this time—and steered me toward the stairs. When I went into my room, he followed.

"Quent, I'm very tired."

"Too bad," Quent said bluntly, and shut and locked the door. "You can sit down or lie down, but I'm not going out of here till I know what's wrong."

"Nothing's wrong."

"Bull. Something happened today I don't know about. Why aren't you telling me?"

"Why should I? Why do you want to know?" Quent did a double take and I thrust my arm out, instinctively, to hold him off. "No, I mean it. Why have you—gotten so involved in helping me like this? You don't even know me, except for meeting me at some party that I can't remember." His jaw dropped, but I went on, talking very fast. "Don't trust anybody. Not without proof, you said. How do I know you're who you say you are?"

The air rang with silence.

"You don't," Quent said at last. "Any more than I have proof you're the girl that I remember. *You* don't even have a passport, do you? I just remembered what it felt like to hold you when we danced, two years ago. If you don't remember that—for some things, there *is* no proof. You just have to trust your sense. Or senses."

He turned to the door, clicked the key in the lock, turned back. "I have a college friend who lives on the other side of London. I'll go stay with him tonight, I think. You'll have to decide for yourself what your feelings are about me. Tomorrow—" He stopped for a moment, then went on. "I'll be at Solange's tomorrow night, at the same time. If you decide you do still want my help, meet me there."

He was gone.

I sat for several minutes staring after him. At last I rose and limped to the door and turned the key. And stood for several moments resting my head against the frame until my eyes had cleared.

When I straightened, one thing out of all the unanswered questions was very clear. *Decide what your feelings are about me*, Quent had said. I didn't know who he was, or whether I should trust him. But I could no longer deny that I was more than half in love.

11

When I awoke next morning my body was one big ache.
My mind and emotions felt black and blue as well. I lay
on the lumpy bed staring at the ceiling cracks, trying to
make order of my thoughts and of the day.

Better to concentrate on the day's schedule. The
less I thought about feelings, the better off I'd be. But
what schedule? I'd tried every lead I could think of.

Something in a corner of my mind laughed deri-
sively. *You're Gabe Langham's daughter, aren't you?
Come on! How does Gabe tackle a dead-end situation
when he's tracking leads?* All these years I'd been around
him when he wrote, not paying much attention, taking
for granted the trips, the ever-present pocket notebook,
the manuscripts that emerged, seemingly effortlessly, from
the typewriter. They were simply the work Dad did, just
as other mothers and fathers disappeared into offices to
perform whatever mysterious tasks took place there. Yet
there must be a method of approaching book research
professionally, just as there were methods and routines
for preparing for gymnastics competition.

I focused hard, trying to conjure up any conversations I'd had with Dad about books and writing. Lists, that was it. Dad always started out by organizing his ideas into working lists. Out of nowhere, the words popped up into my consciousness. *People.* Dad started by making a list of the people who could give him information. And subdivided it according to how best to contact each. *Places.* The place where the crime or other event occurred. Places that must be seen quickly before clues vanished. Places that must be seen when conditions were the same, so that the component parts suggested possibilities. *Objects*—that were evidence; that could suggest things; that could provide information. . . .

My mind was racing too fast for me to keep things straight. I jumped up, heedless of my aching ankle, and rummaged rapidly for pen and paper.

I   PEOPLE WHO CAN PROVIDE INFORMATION
  A) Who I can reach by phone (are phones safe to use? tapped?)
    — *editor)*
    — *publisher)*   *(Try them all again!)*
    — *agent)*   *(phone McCausland & see if she's heard anything)*
  B) People to see in person
    — *dept. of customs/immigration?*
    — *police station in WC 1 district*
  C) People to write to for info.
    — *can't think of any!*
  D) People I don't know how to contact
    — *experts in terrorist activities in Britain*
  E) *Bystanders or witnesses (to what?)*
  F) *Associates of persons named above*

II PLACES WHERE INFO/CLUES ARE AVBL.

A) Places to check out
   — *Hatchards' Book Store, Piccadilly*
   — *Bank Dad usually goes to (Piccadilly next to Ritz)*
   — *Savoy Hotel!!*

B) Places where things happened
   — *Savoy, again (doorman, bartender, head-waiter, elevator men)*
   — *Heathrow airport (in case of kidnapping)*
   — *go back to where things happened to me? (Parliament Square where I was pushed; pub where I met Marla)*

C) Places to see under same conditions (time of day etc.) as when incident happened (what incident?) . . . . ZILCH!!!

D) Places where info's avbl.
   — *newspaper offices*
   — *police*
   — *libraries*
   — *British equiv. of CIA? FBI?*

E) Places Dad hung out.

I had to stop there and really think. Then suddenly I was scribbling quickly.

   — *Savoy*
   — *Covent Garden Market*

That was a mall of fashionable shops now, no longer the "fruit & veg." wholesale market Dad had loved. But he'd told me, hadn't he, what a wonderful "urban renewal project" the conversion was? And how fascinating that it existed, all chic boutiques and high priced merchandise, in the middle of a still-decaying neighborhood.

Where else?

> — *Hyde Park (speakers' corner, where soap-box orators hold forth)*
> — *British Museum (esp. Celtic and Viking depts.)*
> — *V & A Museum*
> — *Fortnum & Masons' food dept.*

I was really fishing for straws with some of those, but one thing was certain. If Dad had been on the loose in London, he would have gone where the food was good.

> — *try to find that pub off Fleet St. where newspaper crowd hangs out!*

What next? I frowned. What had Dad said he did after putting together the resource list? *Look for odd coincidences.* And there were plenty! My hand was racing, my handwriting getting worse, my sides hurting because, crazily, I was holding my breath.

> Getting pushed into the street *right after* I'd gone to Scotland Yard.
> The stonewalling I got at *both* embassies—London *and* Madrid.
> Bumping into Marla the way I had—not to

mention her recognizing me.

Being robbed *twice*—first of luggage, then of passport.

The fact that both Dad and I, apparently, were traveling on false passports.

The way *everybody* was pushing me to go home (except Quint).

Running into Quint so many times—and just when I needed him.

The way this time *nobody* knew anything at all about Dad's project. (Usually he told me something, and definitely his editor and/or agent. Was it likely he'd do anything this dangerous without warning *somebody*, if not me?)

I sat back, staring at the scribbled notes, astonished at how much I'd wrought. And the unanswered question kept pounding in my brain: What was on this paper, what was buried somewhere in my unconscious, that was making me so dangerous to so many people?

There was no use sitting there chewing that one over. I knew exactly what Dad would tell me. Even intuition, when it came, needed to be checked out by rational gathering and analysis of facts. And if intuition *didn't* come, the rational gathering was the only way to prompt it.

Dad would say, "Find a working hypothesis that can become your latitude and longitude to measure by."

I wasn't even close to being able to do that. But I could start checking out the persons and places I'd just put on the list.

Dad started with people, but I was short on people.

Well, I'd do what I could.

I pulled my clothes on, curled my hair. Since I'd been recognizably Sarah when I'd been pushed yesterday, I'd be safer going out as Ellen.

Thinking that way meant I was ruling out the possibility of Quent's involvement, didn't it? The realization startled me. *Or was I just not facing it?*

At any rate, I had until dinnertime to make up my mind. In the meantime Quent was gone, I did not know where.

I had breakfast in the Carr-Saunders cafeteria, feeling shaky. I counted my remaining British money, wondering what I was going to do when it ran out. How could I cash Sarah's travel checks or even convert my American money with Ellen's passport? Or use Sarah's credit card, if asked for identification?

Clutching my bag, hobbling on Ellen's shoes, I went out to catch a bus. Which was closest, the Savoy or Piccadilly? I could get a bus straight down Tottenham Court Road and Charing Cross into the Strand. Checking the Savoy again was a slight hope, but I was ready to grasp at straws.

In my Carnaby Street clothes and bouncing hair, I went up to the hall porter's desk; he looked at me blankly. "May I assist you, miss?"

"I came back to see if you'd thought of anything about my father." When he looked puzzled, I swept my hair back from my face with both my hands.

"I beg your pardon, I did not recognize . . . The—ah, change of style makes quite a difference."

"I thought I'd surprise Dad when I see him," I said glibly. "Don't tell anyone."

"Certainly, miss. And I regret that I have no further information for you. I took the liberty of checking with registration, and your father has not been here at all since last year. And I made enquiries of the other staff. No one has seen him."

"You didn't say—"

"I made no reference to you, since you wished your presence here to be a surprise."

I thanked him and turned away, deflated. I'd better find a mirror in the Ladies' Room and restore my Ellen image. I went down the carpeted stairs toward the luxurious facilities that I remembered, then stopped as I passed an open doorway. The writing room. The writing room, where hardly anybody ever went, although it was possible to have tea served there if you wished. I went inside, and it was like an Edwardian stage set, perfectly appointed, empty. Spindle-legged chairs were pulled up to dainty desks stocked with blotting sheets, pen holders, inkwells, writing paper. *Writing paper*, which any passer-through could pick up and use.

I'd just had proof, hadn't I, of how easily one could come through here with altered looks and be unrecognized? And Dad prided himself on his nondescript appearance.

I pocketed a sheet of paper for future comparison, thanking fortune in yesterday's fall none of the precious evidence had dropped from my bag.

From the Savoy to Piccadilly. I walked to save money, up through Trafalgar Square, past Canada House. (Was Quent there, pulling strings?) Past Piccadilly Circus with its fountain of Eros and its international hodgepodge of students. Could I melt into them if I needed to?

In Piccadilly was Hatchards' bookstore, which Dad patronized, and the branch of Barclay's Bank where he cashed checks. The bookstore came first. New novels and non-fiction were stacked in its bow windows, and a white-haired English lady presided over the front room. I showed her Dad's picture. She shook her head.

Downstairs was the paperback department, where Dad had a habit of going broke. No one there recognized the picture, either. I saw a lurid paperback cover pinned to the display by the cash register and had a bright idea. "Do you have any books on terrorist activities? I have to do a term paper for school."

"Oh, yes, ever so many. There's interest, you know, because of what's happening in Belfast. What aspect of terrorism are you most interested in? You're not sure exactly? Best I turn you over to the gentleman who's our expert on the question."

The man—young, black-haired—produced book after book on everything from the history of terrorist movements to a survey of international terrorism in the past two decades. I bought five, despite the dent the purchase made in my wallet.

"There's a lift, if you'd like to use it," the young man said, noticing my limp. I rode up in the elevator gratefully. The door opened onto the back room where history and travel books were kept. It occurred to me that I should acquire a London map, and I was heading toward a counter when a display on a counter island stopped me dead.

Books on London life for the literate-inclined tourist. *Dad's* book on London, written a few years ago, but only recently available in paper.

I picked a copy up, my fingers shaking. No picture of Dad either in or on it; his British as well as his American publishers honored that insistence. *A writer always needs a premise and a primary source*, Dad had said. What better primary source than Dad's own work, what better premise than that his book was the door into "his London."

I bought a copy and went out, feeling as if I were carrying Pandora's box, into the street.

The bank was a few blocks away. I went there next. Amid the wrought-iron and gilt, the red lacquer and black Chinoiserie, the gracious gray-haired lady at the Enquiries desk looked at Dad's picture and then took it around the International Department/Currency Exchange. No one remembered him.

I needed then to sit down with my lists again and with the books. And I felt safest in a crowd. So I went back to Harrod's with its milling throngs and comfortable seating, found a secluded space, and settled down.

I learned one thing, quite quickly, that I hadn't known before. I'd never *really* read Dad's books. A whole different dimension began to emerge of him and of his London. After an hour I was bleary-eyed, excited and ashamed.

My "working list" was about to expand in all directions.

People to see in person? There was an old man who brought bird seed every day to the land and water fowl in St. James' Park. Apparently he and Dad were "park pals" of long standing. There was the "fruit & veg" man at the wholesale warehouse near Covent Garden. He had been a street kid and petty hoodlum in the East End, and

Dad's book devoted a whole chapter to him, no names mentioned. There was a flower lady with a pushcart in Old Bond Street. There was a bookie in a betting shop off Leicester Square.

People to write to? There were all the persons Dad thanked in his introduction to the London book—persons whose contributions were unspecified but clearly very real. And Dad's book, I'd discovered with chagrin, had whole sections devoted to London's underworld and mob connections.

There were places, in fact, where the book almost screamed out for a sequel, detailing all the illicit things Dad merely hinted at or touched on lightly. Why hadn't I noticed that and asked about it? I knew the answer. Because I took Dad, his talent and his books for granted.

I jerked out my earlier list and started making notes on it like mad. See those people. Check with the publisher for addresses of persons in the dedication. Newspaper offices—I could find out what reporters might know Dad, find out who had written articles on terrorism.

Suddenly the possibilities were multiplying. Clues? I'd thought I hadn't any, but I did. The note that I'd thought had come from the Savoy—maybe other hotels used that same paper. Could I track down the manufacturer? Investigative reporters at any newspaper could tell me how. That torn scrap of paper from the suitcase—I should buy a map and explore every inch of WC 1 on it for a *gton Close.*

And places? Places! Why had I forgotten how Dad laughed over the pelicans at St. James's Park? Why hadn't I known he always spent Sunday mornings feeding coots and loons and swans from the bridge? And how many times had I heard Dad speak of the impressionist paintings at the Tate Gallery, or the special world-in-miniature of Kew Gardens?

I sat up, struck by something. If you wanted to consider cross references and coincidences, Kew Gardens cropped up remarkably often in Dad's book. Even in the chapters on the underworld. Kew Gardens, conveniently receiving plants and other materials from around the world, conveniently on the Thames, which so often had been a smugglers' highway.

There was another place mentioned in the book that also triggered an alarming, illuminating line of thought. The little camera supply place near the Savoy. Cameras. Pictures. Dad didn't allow his picture taken. *I* had a picture of him in my wallet.

What did I know that could make me so dangerous? I knew that Dad had gone to Torremolinos as Mr. Walter Brown. I knew Dad was very interested in, and disturbed by, terrorist activities and possible underworld exploitation of them. *I knew what Dad looked like. I knew who he was.*

I had my working hypothesis now, didn't I? That Dad was on the trail of a terrorist/underworld network, and that his being Gabriel Langham made that especially dangerous—so dangerous that, either as Gabriel Langham or Walter Brown, he had been kidnapped.

I, and I alone, among those who really knew Dad, was suspicious enough to try to find him. *And fast*, a voice in my head said. But I must now, as I never had before, use Dad's kind of caution. I could not leap into anything more the way I'd leaped into trusting Quint, with no evidence but my own emotions.

Where would I start? With the least likely persons to have underworld affiliations, the bird man and the flower-seller.

St. James's Park was full of people on lunch hour, vying with the retirees for lawn chairs and benches. I bought a sausage roll at the food stall, found a chair being vacated by the water's edge. The coots and loons and mallards begged busily, and pigeons and sparrows competed for crumbs around my feet. I didn't feel afraid here; I blended in with all the other London girls.

Was Dad's one-legged pensioner anywhere around? He was, by the bridge, with sparrows eating out of his hand just as described. It was no work at all to get into conversation. He didn't approve of my feeding the birds bits of sausage roll.

" 'Ere, luv, 'ave some bird seed. That's proper kipper." Soon, to my enchantment, sparrows were clustering on my hands, too.

"My dad knows you," I said over their twittering.

"Does 'e, luv? American, is 'e? Quite the local tourist attraction I am. 'Ave their pitchers taken wi'me t'show the blokes back 'ome." The elderly blue eyes were bright with mischief.

"I have a picture of him, but not with you." I shook the last of the seed onto the ground and produced the photo. He peered at it, after wiping his glass carefully on a dirty kerchief.

"Yerss, bought me a cuppa char once or twice 'e 'as. Yer guv'nor, is 'e?"

"Have you seen him lately?"

"Not t'say seen. 'E breezed by so quick the birds felt the wind of 'im." He shrugged. "Not like 'im, is it?

But then lots of toffs 'aven't time to stop for a jaw w'en they're talking business."

"Business?" I seized on it. "He wasn't alone, then?"

"Nah, not this time." The old man chuckled. "Like seein' the Dook wiv the stablehand, but lotsertime silver consorts wiv tin in the business way, don't it?"

He could not give me a description of Dad's companion other than, "Not a gent. Not 'arf."

Now there were two people who had seen Dad in London. I rushed past Marla's uncertainty and concentrated on the fact that the man seen had been out in public, circulating, not a captive. That would indicate Dad had come to England on his own—probably rushing off after a lead. Leaving luggage stripped to anonymity so he could not be traced.

Why the warning note, my mind shouted. Because there was a covert operation trying, thus far unsuccessfully, to kidnap him? Because I was asking too many questions—about Gabriel Langham, or about whoever he had become? Why was I being followed? Why had I been pushed?

Stick to the lists and things that could be done. That was the surest way of finding answers.

The plump flower-seller with the face like wrinkled tissue and talcum powder twinkled at me from behind thick glasses. "Ah, he's a lovely man, he is. Bought some flahrs from me last week. Haven't see him since. Ta, dearie."

It took me a while to find the "fruits & veg." stall near

Covent Garden. I found myself squeezing through a maze of rabbit-warren streets so narrow that automobiles were parked up on the sidewalk. Gaunt city cats rooted among the garbage cans. There were no other women walking here, only men with sly faces, and I felt afraid. I passed market pubs closed at this hour, a head shop selling drug paraphernalia and magazines that would be banned at home. There it was, the stall Dad has described, half inside warehouse, half sidewalk bins under tattered awnings.

"Want sumfin, doll?"

I shook my head wordlessly, avoiding his suggestive leer. Toward the back of the inner room a middle-aged man with a ferrety face and battered cap was ripping the tops off crates of Jaffa oranges. His left eye had a cast. Was he—? I squeezed past the stacks of produce and produced Dad's picture.

I could not have mistaken the instant recognition on the man's face. Nor the fear, even though both were swiftly masked. "Never saw the bloke." He shot a quick, surreptitious look around and repeated loudly, "Never saw 'im." He jerked a heavy carton from the top of a stack, narrowly missing my head. "Get goin'. Customers not allowed in 'here."

I stumbled into Covent Garden square and dropped down on the steps of the church. My legs were weak. The man had looked at Dad's picture, and he'd been afraid. And so had I.

It was teatime now; my throat was parched and I ached all over. In half an hour the business crowds would be homeward bound, but right now the plaza around Covent Garden was practically deserted. The old glass-roofed market was a chic shopping center now. Wouldn't there be tea shops or snack bars or something in with the boutiques? There were. I sat on a wrought-iron chair at a glass-topped table and had strong English tea and wonderful almond tarts called Maids of Honor. I should be poring over the books I'd bought. Or even the map, looking for a place in WC1 called *gton Close*. But I could not keep my thoughts off Quent. Or Dad. What was Quent doing? Had he given up on me entirely, or was he tracking clues in his own fashion? Who was he, really, and what was I going to do about meeting him tonight? Was it safe? Was Dad safe?

I was beginning to wonder whether there was really any such thing as safety. Or if it mattered.

It was time I went home before I started getting really crazy. Not home; to Carr-Saunders, I corrected myself dully. I had to get off my ankle and clean up and decide what I was going to do about Quent.

I came out of Covent Garden Market into the late slanting light, and I saw my father.

He had his back to me, and he was walking rapidly across the pale stones toward the north side of the square. One moment I was just staring blankly, and the next I was running across the space between us as swiftly as my ankle and the uneven stones beneath it would allow. He disappeared from sight into King Street, and I hurried after. He had disappeared. Where? A side road jutted off at right angles, and I crossed toward it, just avoiding a produce truck, my heart pounding.

There was the tall figure, a block and half ahead and heading north. *You can't be sure*, that voice in my head said. *You haven't seen his face*. That was the investigative side of my father in me; skeptical, objective. But Dad had an intuitive side, too, and I was more and more aware that I had inherited it. That was what had taken me to Spain, wasn't it, had made me know when I saw Dad's suitcase, had brought me to London against all rational advice. Had made me trust in Quent. Made me argue now, *It's Dad build, Dad's way of walking, Dad's tilt of head. Those are things that it's hard work to change. There are tiny traits that might escape outsiders, but not those really close. Did I know I placed my weight slightly off center, till my gymnastics coach showed me how it made me prone to fall? Does Dad know he turns his head a millimeter whenever he tells a lie?*

All the while I was running, half stumbling, mechanically using the techniques I'd learned to maintain balance. And the figure in front of me kept getting farther away.

A streetlight changed, and he ignored it. So did I. He turned a corner. When I reached it, he was striding around through a Regency square. I found a gate in the square's wrought-iron fence, opening onto a diagonal path, and flung myself into it, shortening the distance between us to a full block.

We were in a part of London strange to me—prim white stone houses, shabby-genteel, bearing Bed & Breakfast signs in many windows. I glanced at a street sign and realized we were in Bloomsbury, "literary London," so Carr-Saunders could not be far away. It was growing darker, and lamps were going on in windows. The streets were almost deserted; I could hear the tap-tap of Ellen's shoe heels on the pavement.

Almost, I called out, but something held me back.

Insecurity? Premonition of danger? I do not know. He crossed the next street just as a heavy truck lumbered through the cross street after him, cutting him from view.

When the truck moved on, there was nobody in sight. I ran, literally ran, to the corner and peered in all directions through the twilight. The earth could have opened and swallowed him up whole.

There were no stores, hotels or public places into which he might have turned. There were only houses, closed, remote. I stood on the corner, staring helplessly, as hot tears stung my eyes. And the twilight deepened, and lights kept going on, but I could see nothing inside those tight enclosures because of that damned English habit of shutting the curtains at lamp-lighting time.

How long I stood there I do not know. At last I became conscious that it was dark, and I was bone-tired. And very hungry.

Dinner. Quent. Quent was waiting for me at Chez Solange, and suddenly all I wanted was to be there, to tell him I had seen my father and hear what he could suggest. I no longer doubted him. The leap of faith had been taken.

With my last money I took a cab to Leicester Square.

Quent was sitting at the same banquette, his head turned so he could see the door. He didn't think I was coming. I knew that in the moment I saw him, before he saw me. He was sitting there with the menu still unopened, waiting with dwindling hope.

Bedraggled as I was, in my Ellen-hair and Ellen-clothes that didn't fit the restaurant's Edwardian opulence, I went toward him.

12

"You can't be sure it was your father," Quent said, much later.

I shook my head doggedly. "I can." I glanced toward him, then away, feeling myself flushing. "Do you really not want me to trust my intuition?"

Quent laughed aloud, and his hand covered mine. "You've made your point. I won't argue. What do we do now, compare notes on our accomplishments today?"

"We eat. I have a lot to tell you, but I'd better do it later. I'm famished."

Dinner was heavenly, but I couldn't tell you what it was. The previous night's food I remember, and remember that it seemed like cardboard. But this wasn't like the night before at all.

We walked out into Cranbourne Street holding hands. I was limping, of course, and Quent put his arm around me to help me across the street, and he didn't take the arm away. Above us, the Talk of the Town nightclub sign lit up the night.

"I wish I were taking you dancing," Quent said. "I wish I were taking you to the theater. There's such great theater here, and you aren't seeing it."

"We will. After." I did not even let myself think of the possibility that Dad would not be found. "I wonder if I should go back to Scotland Yard," I said aloud. "Now that I've seen him. Now that I *know* he's here."

"You still can't give them any concrete proof that there's anything wrong, any reason they should get involved."

"I can show them my black-and-blue mark from getting pushed before a bus."

"You don't know—" Quent felt me stiffen and gave me a swift squeeze. "I'm not trying to start an argument, just pointing out it *could* have been an accident. And that we still have nothing solid to prove anyone's in danger."

"I haven't told you yet. One man I hunted up, out of Dad's book, looked scared when he saw Dad's picture. And denied he'd even seen him. When Dad's written up accounts of whole conversations that they've had over the years! He practically threw me out. Quent, he was afraid of something!"

Quent grew alert. "Where was this?" When I told him, he looked appalled. "What were you doing prowling around that neighborhood? It's not a safe place for a girl at any time. It's gang territory. There's all sorts of criminal activity. And weapons."

"Terrorists?"

"Don't go imagining things. Just stay away from there."

"Unless I've got my sense of geography completely scrambled, we're headed there right now."

"Good Lord." Quent jerked to a stop. "That's what happens when I start concentrating. I simply headed toward Carr-Saunders the shortest way without thinking about the route. We'd better get a cab."

Cabs, however, proved to be in short supply. "It doesn't matter," I said. "You're with me now. Let's just get home, so I can tell you—"

"Hold it. We can cut through this street, I think, and come out on Charing Cross Circus and catch a bus." Quent was holding me close, guiding me, hurrying me. The steet was very dark, and the sidewalk was uneven. I tripped over my own feet, hung onto him and righted myself.

"Can we catch our breath a minute?" We were going along the blank back wall of a theater, and a fixture by the stage door made a pool of light. We went toward it, and I steadied myself with one hand on the wall while Quent checked my ankle, shaking his head.

"Better put a stretch bandage on that tomorrow. Think you can make it to the bus stop?"

"Of course I can!" I said indignantly, straightening. To prove it, I stepped out before he was ready.

Crash—

I didn't know what it was, I only knew that Quent had flung himself toward me, knocking us both down. Away from the circle of light. Away from—

"Stay down," Quent whispered tensely as I struggled. Sensing his urgency, I was silent. After a moment we could hear, faint but unmistakable, footsteps receding high above us.

"Someone on the roof. He's gone now," Quent said quietly. He got up, brushed himself off, helped me up. We stared at the block of stone on the sidewalk where I had been standing.

Before I knew what was happening, Quent swept me up in his arms. "Shut up," he muttered, striding around the theater. "And act hurt. Show should be getting out, so we ought to be able to steal a taxi."

Back at Carr-Saunders, Quent insisted on carrying me up to my room. "If people think you're hurt worse than you are, good," he said flatly, setting me on the bed and locking the door firmly. The BBC cushion of sound blared on.

"Quent, you don't think—"

"I think you've convinced me. That was one coincidence too many, even if Scotland Yard would say there's no proof it wasn't an accident." His mouth twisted. "I hope you noticed this time I had an alibi."

"What I'm noticing," I said soberly, "is that this time it was 'Ellen' who almost got killed. Not 'Sarah.'"

We looked at each other. Then Quent swung toward the door. "I'll be back in less than five minutes. Lock the door after me, and don't open it for anything until you hear my voice."

I heard myself say, with an attempt at lightness, "You weren't afraid to leave me in this room last night. You were way across town."

"No, I wasn't," Quent said tightly. "I only told you that to make you think. Anyway, things have changed now. If somebody's put 'Sarah' and 'Ellen' together, he probably knows exactly where you are. Propriety or no propriety, I'm sleeping on the floor of your room tonight."

Neither of us slept much. I awoke at dawn to find Quent also awake. I got out my lists, and Quent took notes. "I can check with the newspapers and the police about recent terrorist activities here. And the money laundering. An Oxford ID and a research paper to write can get me pretty far. Come to think of it, one of the guys in my dorm is the son of one of the Home Office bigwigs. Maybe I can talk to him. And our embassy may be some help on finding out what suspicious characters are in town right now. I'll try to find out what your fruit-and-veg. man could have been afraid of. And that character eavesdropping from behind the racing form sounds worth checking out."

"I'll check some of the other places Dad mentioned. There's Kew Gardens and the Zoo."

"*You* stay *here*. I mean it, Sarah. You don't have to prove to me that you've got guts; and what's the use of our getting closer to your father if you end up splattered on the sidewalk before we find him?"

I don't know which jolted me the most, Quent's bluntness or the matter-of-fact way he took for granted that I was in danger. After breakfast I let him escort me back to my room and even check beneath the bed. "That suitcase isn't big enough for anyone to hide in," I said caustically as he inspected it. Quent just looked at me.

"It's big enough to hold a bomb. Or haven't you looked at the photographs in that book on terrorist weapons you bought?"

When Quent left, I locked the door behind him. I sat down to make sense out of my notes, then to read the book he mentioned, very conscious of the passing of time.

It was so frustrating to be doing nothing, only waiting! There were so many loose ends. We still did not know where *-gton Close* was. None of the experts I'd talked to had thought it worth offering suggestions. That, at least, was one thing I could work on. I spread my London map out and began poring over the area, but could find nothing. So many London alleys and cul-de-sacs were thought too unimportant to be shown on maps.

Noon came, and one o'clock, and still no Quent. By ten of two, common sense—or hunger—was winning out over paranoia. The Carr-Saunders cafeteria was closing in ten minutes, and what, after all, could happen to me there? I unlocked the door, feeling ridiculous about the whole thing, and went upstairs.

Everything was so innocuous. A few students lounged over half-empty coffee cups, deep in talk. By the windows two others were playing chess. A tired-looking elderly woman served me soup, bread and cheese, and I sat at the table nearest the cashier, feeling vaguely that Quent would be mollified if I stayed close to somebody official.

After a while the girl I'd seen yesterday at the front desk came in, got tea and joined the intellectual discussion. When she rose to leave, she passed my table, hesitated, then came over. "Aren't you Ellen Robards?"

I nodded warily.

"There's a message at the desk for you. I saw it when I came on duty."

Quent must have been trying to get in touch with me—which, come to think of it, was odd. I said, "Thanks," briefly, and went down to the lobby.

It wasn't from Quent. Somebody had scribbled down, on one of those "While You Were Out" forms, a telephoned message for me from Marla Finch at Esterley and James. "Tell Sarah I've seen her dad. Meet me Russell Square 5 p.m. for more info."

For a minute I just stood there blankly, afraid to believe, yet wanting to so much. Then I looked at the clock and was galvanized to action. No use phoning Marla; I could not talk freely at Carr-Saunders's open booth. And even without Quent's warning, I was afraid to leave the building all alone.

If I didn't phone, how would I know the message was from her and not a trap?

Quent had to get back here before five. I searched my mind frantically for the places he had mentioned going, looked up numbers, dumped my coins out on the telephone ledge and started dialing. Canadian Embassy, Scotland Yard, Hatchards—even, so help me, the Home Office. At each place the answer was the same. No, Mr. Quenton Robards was not there now. Yes, if he appeared, they would be happy to tell him his sister needed him at once.

Back to my room; lock myself in; pace the floor. My ankle wasn't hurting any more. Time was going by, and Quent did not come. At ten minutes of five I went back down. No Quent; no messages. I made a call to Esterley and James after all. A bored operator said Miss Finch was not there.

Of course: she would have had to leave by now to get to Russell Square. Why Russell Square, anyway? Near where she lived? Or near where she'd seen Dad? At least it was not far from here. I could not stand still; I kept pacing back and forth from telephone to door, and all the while the clock kept ticking. Then the clock struck the hour with a metallic *ping*, and I knew, quite suddenly and clearly, that whatever the risk—of being followed; of being lured into a trap—I *had* to take this chance.

I went out the door, out the steps, into the street.

Students were beginning to saunter home, and the after-tea-wait-for-beer crowd was lingering around the pub on the far corner. No one looked at me, and no one followed. I went, as quickly as I could, zigzagging through residential streets toward Russell Square. Looking over my shoulder when I dared, avoiding tight places, watching what reflections I found in windows. Hoping that *perhaps*, just perhaps, this was really on the level.

Russell Square was green and bright with spring, and there were children playing here and there. No tour buses, no waiting bus lines, no queue for taxis—it was between-hours here, and the square slumbered peacefully in the late afternoon light. I sat down on a metal bench beneath a tree.

There was no sign of Marla. I peered across the square, glanced over my shoulder, thinking how useful for spying compact mirrors must have been. I'd seen that done once in a movie on late-night TV. But this was the nineteen-eighties, and I sat tensely in this peaceful place, listening and watching . . . seeing nothing out of the ordinary. Hearing nothing but the birds.

Nothing rustled behind me, nothing moved, and yet all at once my scalp began to prickle. I shifted cautiously, to steal a glance. Before I could move my head, something pressed against my shoulder blade at heart level.

"I wouldn't," a voice murmured quietly.

Not Dad's voice. Not Marla's.

I froze, scarcely breathing, and the voice went on, whispery, conversational, "Just get up, ever so easy, and you won't get hurt." A man's voice. A London voice. Automatically, I obeyed.

For an instant the gun shifted. Don't ask me why I didn't run. I simply couldn't. Maybe I was afraid to. I don't know. What I do know is that I stepped forward slightly, and as I did so the man was around the bench and right beside me, half behind me, his arm around me familiarly and the gun somehow pressed against my side.

It was the man from the pub. I knew the loud check of his jacket sleeve and the odd cheap green of his trousers and his heavy shoes. Shoes with thick crepe soles, so that he could come up behind me and I wouldn't even know. I didn't dare turn toward his face, but I knew if I did I would see the distinctive odd-shaped head that I remembered.

All this went through my brain like a reel of film, while we were moving steadily through Russell Square. It was late afternoon, daylight, in the middle of a public place, and I was being kidnapped, and nobody cast a glance in our direction. Almost, I could have laughed. No way could I have screamed.

The bottom had dropped out of my stomach, but my legs kept moving on automatic pilot, and my brain kept clicking. Keep calm, it said. Sooner or later someone will see. Sooner or later he'll make one false move, and you must be ready. You must not, dare not, make one false move yourself.

And so we walked, like any London couple, out of Russell Square and through the quiet streets. The white fronts of the buildings gleamed in the late sun.

"Where are you taking me?" I asked at last, quite calmly.

"Never you mind. You've asked enough questions already."

So this was because of all those questions. How odd that my quarry took them seriously when Scotland Yard did not. "Asking questions can be dangerous," Dad had said once, grinning. "It stirs up dust, and all kinds of things lurking in dark corners." A curious, fatalistic stillness settled over me.

I was turned into a narrow street that was half an alley, turned again into a wider, dead-end courtyard rimmed with gracious houses. Wrought-iron fenced a minute square in the center. A London street sign was attached to it.

Covington Close.

We went round the square to a corner house at the far end, the corner house of a long row of connected houses. I remember that there were seven steps and that the paint on the stone was very white and that there were closed shutters at the downstairs windows. My legs were like lead, and the rest of me was shivering

The man shifted his gun to the center of my back and rang the bell.

It was opened almost at once by a slight, dark young man. He knew my captor but was startled to see me. I saw that, even though the surprise was quickly veiled. He looked faintly foreign, though he was dressed in impeccable English fashion. When he spoke, it was in Oxford English, and I almost fainted.

In the front of his mouth a gold tooth gleamed.

It could not be . . . it had to be . . . yet he was saying, with authoritative displeasure, "What do you mean by this preposterous stunt, Piggott? I told you we'd take care of this particular problem."

"Been hearin' that an' hearin' that, haven't we? It's what you were brought to London for, wasn't it? But I've been shadowing you shadowing 'er for days now. She's still asking, and you 'aven't done nothing. Makes a bloke wonder, don't it? So I thought we'd drop in unexpected-like, and see what your Mr. Big has to say now that we've got the girl."

"He will not be pleased," Gold-tooth retorted. "Especially if it turns out you made a mistake and she knows nothing."

"Don't know that yet, do we?" the tout said easily. Their eyes locked. Numbly I wondered if the gun now threatened not only me but the Spanish man as well.

Nothing changed, yet somehow Gold-tooth seemed to grow larger, and somehow menacing, like a cat relaxed yet utterly alert. The tout knew it, too. The balance of power had shifted. I stood quiet, every nerve straining for the moment when the false move should come.

It didn't. Gold-tooth said silkily, "Go on upstairs. He's in his office." We moved up the stairs, a curious procession, me in the lead. Up two flights and to the left, to a near-cornered door. Mr. Big's office was in the rear.

Gold-tooth knocked. A male voice, gruff and impatient, snapped, "Who is it?"

"Esteban, sir. Mr. Piggott has returned without appointment and has brought a friend." There was a curious twist to the last word.

"Very well. Show him in." There was no threat to

the tone, yet somehow it had the effect of great power. Behind me I heard Mr. Piggott shift his weight. Goldtooth—Esteban—straightened his jacket and his right hand surreptitiously brushed his trouser pocket. A little voice in my head said, *In a movie, he'd have a gun there.* Only this was no movie.

Then Esteban turned the door handle, and the door swung inward, and the whole picture shifted. This was no Mafia den out of the late movies. It was an ordinary office, rather small, with commonplace gray and green metal furniture everywhere.

"Mr. Maguire, Mr. Piggott and the lady are here," Esteban said levelly. I looked toward the far end of the room.

There was a battered wooden desk before the window. Behind it, in a swivel chair turned toward the window, a large man sat. He was relaxed, yet not as Esteban was; more like a sleeping bear. The waning light cast him half in shadow; yet even though I could see little, my inner picture changed again. Here was power, power great enough that it flowed from this man, Maguire, without his turning and clashed with the power of Piggott and his gun. I was suddenly quite sure that Esteban had a weapon covering us both.

Piggott sensed it too. Piggot was braced—to challenge, not to run. He said, as he had before, "Been makin' us wonder, Mr. Maguire, why you haven't taken steps yet about this bird that's poking her nose into things. Not quite what we expected when we started doing business with you, is it? So it seems to my people it's time you identified her properly and cleared up what's going on."

Mr. Maguire did not move a muscle. "It seems to us

it's time you delivered your merchandise as agreed. Time's money, and you're wasting mine."

Mr. Piggott smiled. "Oh, we're ready to deliver. Goods were put in the place specified today, all nice and tidy. Only we're not sure how wise it is to let you make the pick-up, you see, till you clear up this matter and back your credentials, you might say. So you'd better un-glue yourself, Mr. Maguire, and cast a butcher's eye, as the saying goes. Was this girl's asking round for you coin-cidence, or is she on to you? Because that would mean trouble for us, y'see, as well as you."

He pushed me forward. Mr. Maguire swung his feet down, and the chair squeaked as it swiveled. We faced each other, and I felt the room grow hot, grow cold. The voice roared, "You damn fool, I've never seen this girl before!"

But the man looking at me with deliberate blank-ness was my father.

13

My known world was spinning on its axis. It tilted, righted itself, and swung into a queer kind of balance. My mind, crazily, watched from a long way off, was not involved at all.

My father was very much involved. It was like that passage in the Bible about another case af assumed identity: "The hands are the hands of Esau, but the voice is the voice of Jacob." The voice I heard was the voice of a strange "Mr. Maguire," but it was Dad's temper, Dad's vocabulary coming out in those alien tones. "You idiotic, incompetent English fool, snatching a girl off the street just because she's carrying around a photograph you *think* resembles me!"

His voice was heavy with scorn. "If this is a sample of the 'safety precautions' your operation takes, it makes me think twice about doing business with you at all. Do you think your superiors are going to be pleased about *that?*"

Mr. Piggott was a cornered ferret, but a vicious one. "We'll see about that, won't we?" he said softly. "When we find out who this bird is and what she's up to. Not to mention what you're really up to, Mr. Maguire. Can't take you on faith just because you come to Limey with a roll of U.S. currency, can we?"

It *was* a matter of money laundering, then.

"So we'll just have to wait and see whether your money's as clean as you claim it is. That's part of the safety precautions my superiors take, y'see. I don't know about yours—"

Dad's "Maguire" voice said, just as quietly, "In my operation, *I* make the decisions, and I don't like being forced to deal with sublieutenants." A dull red stained Piggott's cheeks, but Dad went on in that same dangerous calm. "I came from Spain to look you up, because I understood you had merchandise to sell. I gave you excellent credentials, not only from my organization but from ETA, and I do not care, any more than will my colleagues, to have them doubted. Nor do I care to be kept waiting." The voice bellowed into a roar. "What the hell do you expect me to do, stand around listening to the hurdy-gurdy play in lilac time?"

The skin on my scalp suddenly went tight. There had been a day when Dad had roared because he was alarmed about my safety. A picture flared in my mind: Dad splitting the air with profanity when I was ten and he caught me tightrope-walking the deck railing pretending to be Wonder Woman. He'd whaled the tar out of me, and the next day he'd taken me downtown and enrolled me for my first gymnastics lesson. He'd yelled at me like this, then.

He'd even yelled some of these same words: *"No-body's telling you that you have to be an old-fashioned little girl, sitting in a corner while the boys have all the fun. Nobody's telling you you have to just stand around listening to the hurdy-gurdy play in lilac time. But drat and blast it, you're my daughter, aren't you? Is it too much to expect you to use the brains the good Lord gave you?"*

I was using them now, furiously. Dad was telling me that I was in danger, that I must use my brains.

He was telling me something more. *Listening to the hurdy-gurdy play in lilac time* . . . that was from a poem I used to love to hear him read aloud. It was by Alfred Noyes, and it was all about London.

"Come down to Kew in lilac-time, it isn't far from London . . ." Kew Gardens, which kept cropping up like a coincidence in Dad's book. Dad was telling me all this had something to do with Kew. Why? What did he expect me to be able to do with the knowledge? I half-closed my eyes, the way I'd have done if I'd really let myself give way to fear. Behind their shutters I strained all my other senses to pick up clues.

The conversation had become a deadly poker game —a struggle for power. Mr. Piggott was demanding that my purse be searched. Dad tried to block it; suddenly must have realized I wasn't afraid of it; capitulated. The Spaniard dumped the contents on the desk, went through a rapid inventory for the benefit of both the others.

"Dark glasses. Eye makeup. Lipstick. Comb. Hairclip. Map of London. Paperback book about terrorist activities." Why had I so stupidly brought that with me? "Wallet containing photograph with slight resemblance to Mr. Maguire and twenty-eight pence in change." *Why* had I brought that picture of Dad with me? "Passport—"

There was a silence. Then Dad's voice, very, very

quiet and calm. "A diplomatic passport. A *Canadian* diplomatic passport. Mr. Piggott, are you beginning to have an idea of the jeopardy into which your impetuosity has placed us?"

Mr. Piggott tried to speak, but Dad cut him off sharply. "This is out of your hands now. I am not going to risk my neck to your ineptitude." He swung round on the Spaniard. "You will copy the pertinent information from the passport. Then you will lock the young lady and her belongings in the end room. The end room," he repeated firmly, as the Spaniard seemed about to protest. "After that you will come back here and verify the passport data by telephone."

"We can't just—" Mr. Piggott started, and again Dad interrupted smoothly.

"Whatever steps are necessary for our safety, we shall take in the morning, after due deliberation. Meanwhile, Mr. Piggott, we shall wait. You will not complete the transaction, you say, until you are assured my currency is untraceable. Very well."

He reached into a file drawer, took out a worn attaché case I had never seen and snapped the catch.

Mr. Piggott's eyes were suddenly avid.

"There it is," Dad said softly. "A quarter of a million dollars in unmarked used bills. Since you guarantee the merchandise has already been placed in the spot agreed, I will permit your associate to transfer the payment to your bank and have it checked. I will remind you that financial offices in the States do not open until two p.m. London time. I will permit this, I say, because while he is waiting for the bills to clear, you and I, Piggott, will remain here together."

Between narrowed eyelids I saw Dad move easily in what could have been a stretch. It brought his right hand closer to where a gun might be. The Spaniard did the same. Mr. Piggott tensed, then sat back in his chair and hoisted his pointed shoes onto the desk. "Very well, guv'nor. We wait."

He lit a cigar elaborately, sent a puff of nauseating smoke toward the ceiling. "Not to worry, say I. Y'don't think I was fool enough to come here without protective backup, do you? No, I had chaps keepin' 'obbo on me, as they say, right up to your front door. And they'll be around till I come out again, all fresh and easy." His tone sharpened. "All the same, *you're* the bloody fool if you're satisfied to leave the girl unguarded and unbound."

"My good ass!" Dad's voice rose to a roar again. "You've just told me your men are watching the front! This is a safe house. I chose it carefully and arranged the rental for these express purposes, and every room has been individually soundproofed. In any event, the building adjoining is all offices now closed up for the night. What do you think our Miss Robards is, a defecting Soviet gymnast who can go capering along a ledge three stories up, like a mountain goat?" He swept an ironic nod in my direction, while my pulses throbbed.

Mr. Piggott blew a smoke ring angrily. The Spaniard took me by the elbows and steered me toward the door. His grip was hard. I stumbled, was propelled past two closed doors. Holding me tightly, he reached around to unlock the third door. Pushed it open. Pushed me in.

It was a small room, high ceilinged, evidently a secretarial office. My guard backed out, pulling the door shut after him. I heard the key turn in the lock.

I heard Dad's voice, three rooms down, ripping more skin off Mr. Piggott. Clearly, that statement about the rooms being soundproofed had been a lie. And a warning. Cautiously, I slipped my shoes off, tiptoed around on the dull brown carpet, making an inspection tour.

Two tall windows, their curtains open. Below them, some ten inches down, a decorative stone ledge about four inches wide ran along the back of all the houses. Below the ledge was a sheer drop into a mews. I drew back, feeling dizzy. In the buildings across the mews, windows were shaded, shuttered or blank; no lights, no signs of life.

In the room were a shabby metal secretary's desk, two chairs, a four-drawer filing cabinet, battered bookcases. A typewriter. A telephone—I dared not risk that. I could be overheard; it could be bugged. I folded up on the floor as the enormity of the situation and my own responsibility crashed over me like a wave.

I had brought this on myself, and on Dad. I, who was so proud of having inherited the Langham intuition, had blundered full tilt into this on the strength of intuition, instinct and just plain hunch. Never, as Dad said, using the brains the good Lord gave me. Oh, I had thought I had. I'd been so proud of my cleverness, hadn't I? But I'd only been halfway to really being "Gabriel's girl." *Gabe* coupled his brilliant intuition with cool, rational brainwork, an ability to look at all angles and weigh all odds, a large dose of caution and just plain common sense. All of which had been spectacularly missing in me up till now.

All of which I'd need, if I was to get myself out of

here and accomplish whatever else Dad was expecting of me. That he *was* expecting something, I had no doubt.

All right, I told myself doggedly, do some rational brainwork. What did I know about this situation? That I would probably be undisturbed in this room until the morning. That the front of the house was being watched. That Dad was exchanging cash—a quarter of a million dollars of clean cash—for some merchandise. That this all had some connection with Kew Gardens.

That Dad wanted me to do something he apparently could not. But what? And then, all at once, it struck me.

Clean cash. Dad *was* involved in money laundering. Merchandise. Weapons of some kind, explosives, hidden in Kew Gardens. Merchandise he was not being allowed to claim until that quarter of a million proved to be unmarked.

And it was not unmarked. That was the only explanation. It meant Dad *was* on the "good guy's" side. I hadn't realized how afraid I'd been about that until now. Dad was trapped here until the money was checked, and once it was? The "merchandise" would vanish from its drop, and he'd be killed. I had learned, from all my hurried reading, the vast resources of these "merchants of death," and the cheapness to them of human life.

Dad's credibility was almost gone, partly because of me. It would be totally gone soon after two p.m. tomorrow. Dad had given me until sometime in the morning to get out of here, find that merchandise he needed as evidence and get him rescued.

Part of me flooded with pride that he trusted my intelligence and resourcefulness, even after the mess I'd made. Part of me longed desperately to be back in childhood, to be able to run to him and have him tell me this was all a dream.

It was no dream. It was, all too chillingly, the very stuff I'd been reading about in that terrorism book. I had to struggle to choke back hysteria. And all the time the voices in the other room went on: Dad's; Mr. Piggott's; the Spaniard's; and presently two other, unidentifiable, English voices. Dad said something about sending out for food. The Spaniard did so by telephone.

Their voices were so clear I was afraid to make a sound. I crept around on the carpet, trying the desk drawers (locked), the filing cabinet (empty). I pulled myself up, noiselessly, went through book after book in the open cases. Nothing—not a scrap of paper, not a note. No hidden compartments, like in old spy stories. I was finishing the last one when I heard the key turn in the lock.

I jammed the book back and sat down hastily. My heart was pounding. Now, as I write this, everything sounds so cut and dried, but it was not. It was like a movie happening in slow motion. The key turned, the door opened silently, and the Spaniard came in. He was carrying a tray with one of those awful stale English-luncheonette sandwiches and a small milk carton. He set it on the desk, selected another key, unlocked the top desk drawer, took out some papers, relocked the drawer and went away. Neither of us spoke. Neither of us even looked at the other. When he was gone, I heard him locking me in again.

He had put the light on while he was in the room and had left it on. Its brightness almost hurt my eyes. For several moments I sat eyeing the greasy sandwich; then hunger overcame my caution, and I ate it gratefully.

143

There was a clock over the door. Its hands stood at twenty-eight minutes after eight. If I was going to get away, I would have to wait untl it was pitch dark, but I could not wait until it was so late that the presence of a young girl on the street would itself be suspicious. And I would have to figure out a way to get into the street without being recognized by Mr. Piggott's "protective back-up." Once out, I would have to think of a place to go. Not back to Carr-Saunders; the call supposedly from Marla indicated that that was no longer safe. I wondered fleetingly what Quent was doing; what he had thought when he returned and found me gone. There was no way he could trace me here.

I might as well improve my mind while I'm waiting for pitch blackness, I thought grimly, and took the terrorism book out of my purse. Maybe I could learn something that would help. So I sat as the clock ticked from eight-thirty to nine, to nine-fifteen, reading about safe houses and dirty money and guns and bombs. Bombs that could be set like a timer-oven. Bombs that exploded when pressed. Bombs of glass and metal and pipe and plastic.

I caught myself, just in time, about to drum my fingers nervously on the metal desk. Then automatically, in nervous movement, my hand moved down and tried the top desk drawer.

It moved.

It had been locked before; I had seen it be relocked; yet something had gone wrong, and it was open. Scarcely breathing, I edged it outward, inch by inch, memories of my bomb-reading whirling through my head.

There was no bomb inside, not even a letter-bomb. There was only paper. Bookkeeping ledger sheets and a folder on Kew Gardens.

I was afraid to take them out onto the desk for fear someone somewhere could see me through the window. So I slid them out carefully; slid with them from the desk chair down onto the floor. There, crouched in a corner, my back to the room, I studied them until my eyes were aching.

The ledgers made no sense at all. I folded the sheets anyway, slipped them in my purse. Then, my heart hammering, I spread out the folder. And all my senses screamed that this was it, this was why Dad had put me in this room, this was what I had been looking for.

The outside of the folder showed pictures of plants in the Royal Botanical Garden, and inside was a map. On the map, just possibly, was a pencil mark. Halfway down the right side of the garden, in the rhododendron dell, was a faint mark that could have been—but mustn't be—a smudge.

In quiet, slow motion, I folded the map and thrust it not into my purse but inside my bra. If I dropped my purse, or lost it, or had to leave it behind me, the map had to come along. I put my shoes in my purse, though, and my stockings. Then, in my bare feet, I eased myself up and over to the light switch; silently I flicked the light out.

It took a few minutes before my eyes adjusted. Then, catlike, I went to the window and checked the lock. It shifted easily. *Please God*, I thought, and tried the window. It slid up without a sound. I was staring out into almost utter blackness.

Faintly, very faintly, there was some moonlight. Just enough to make out the houses opposite and the ledge gleaming palely below me, stretching, thank goodness, in the same pattern onto the next building. But I had been sitting, tense, too long. I dared not move out there yet. Methodically, doggedly, I put myself through limbering-up exercises. And when at last I could half-hear my coach saying "Ready," I looped the long handle of my bag around my neck, sat on the windowsill and swung out first one leg, then the other.

Only rims of light outlined the windows of the room down the hall where Dad's and the others' voices still went on. The windows in between were black. I took hold of the window frame, tested it, and slowly eased myself up to my feet. The stone was rough beneath my bare soles, but my toes found a purchase on it. Found a balance.

I must not look down. I must relax and maintain balance and stay alert and never doubt. Inch by inch, step by step, I edged myself along the ledge toward the next building, not looking back. Not permitting myself to wonder what I would do if there was no way to get into the empty offices in the building next door. If they *were* empty! But they had to be empty. I could not risk being seen, even by rescuers; I dared not risk whatever Dad was up to.

The first window I came to was closed tight, black and shuttered. I found a handhold on the frame, edged my way with difficulty to the flat wall beyond. Six feet more and there would be another window.

It was open.

It was open, and it opened into a dark room. I was not even consciously thinking as—carefully, carefully—

I eased one leg after the other through the opening and slid inside.

I landed on a floor, an uncarpeted floor. The room was dark and empty, except of office furniture, and the door was closed. Everything was silent. *Thank God*, I thought.

Even so, I had to crouch there several minutes, quivering like jelly, before I dared to stand.

14

I was free. And I was safe. Half-safe, I realized. I still had to get out of this building and through the streets, unrecognized.

On my feet, still barefoot and still shaking, I held myself motionless in the corner, out of window-view, and considered the situation. I had scrapes on my bare skin from the building stones, but I was otherwise unhurt. What now? Risk picking up the telephone here on the desk? But who would I call?

The publishers and the agency were closed. I could not risk calling Quent. The police? The embassy? My mind touched the possibilities briefly, skittered away from their earlier disbelief.

This building was so still. There were no sounds from next door. I dared not risk a light, but after an eternity, I eased myself to the door and opened it a crack. It made no sound. A faint light burned in the hall beyond. I drew the door open slowly.

The building had the same layout as the other. Closed doors, back and front, in a row on each side of a narrow corridor, a narrow old-fashioned stairway twisting upward, twisting down. Below was darkness; above was more dim light.

Suddenly, above me distantly came a humming. I froze. Then my senses cleared. It was the familiar, homely sound of a vacuum cleaner being pushed back and forth too fast. Somewhere upstairs a cleaning woman—a "char," Dad's book said they were called here—was "doing up" the offices by night. That was why I'd found that window open. The room's occupant hadn't bothered to close it, knowing the char would catch it. Or else the char herself had propped it open, to "let the room air after cleaning"—and would come back about it later.

If I did not want to get caught, I must get out of here. Everything in me yearned for a friendly, motherly, Selena-like face, but I was too afraid. I strained my ears. The vacuuming seemed to be coming from at least two floors above me. Thank heaven it was not between me and the door. With infinite care I crept to the stairs and started down, flattening myself against the wall.

When a stair tread creaked, I almost screamed. I waited, scarcely breathing. No break in the steady, cheerful vacuum hum. Down again, on tiptoe, testing the treads and easing my weight down slowly. Lower and lower I went into the darkness, my ears alert for the slightest sound.

There was none. I put my feet at last onto the cold marble of the entrance hall and clung to the newel post while I catalogued my surroundings.

A faint glow came down from the floors above, and light arrowed in through the fanlight above the door— enough illumination to reveal old-fashioned double entrance doors with frosted glass and a pair of elaborate carved doors to what had once been double parlors. There were brass nameplates on those doors. *J.C. Carrington, Esq. Monteith-Munro Importers, Ltd.* For a wild moment I wondered if there was a link between these importers and the merchandise Dad was trying to buy.

"He wouldn't have sent me here if it hadn't been safe," I told myself sternly. Or as safe as possible, under the circumstances. Anyway, so far, so good. But how was I to get from here out through the streets unseen? I did not kid myself that there was no one watching.

What I had to rely on—*all* I had to rely on—was Langham ingenuity. And on striking Gabe Langham's balance between intuition and cool reason. I shut my eyes and prayed frantically for inspiration.

I opened my eyes and saw an open door at the far end of the hall.

Was there a back exit? I had not noticed whether the mews behind the row of houses had an opening to another street. I could check. There was no sound anywhere on this lower floor, so I tiptoed toward the open doorway and peered inside. Then my hopes sank. It was not an exit, not even a room, only a "char's storeroom" of cleaning supplies. Pails, mops, brooms, garments hanging on hooks—

The blood started pounding in my temples. I groped for the light cord, and holding it tightly, careful not to pull it, I slid into the storeroom and eased the door tight behind me. Then, only then, did I tug the cord.

The room sprang to life. Tiny, no larger than a big closet, it was used for more than storage. There was a hot plate and a battered tin kettle on a shelf next to thick mugs and a tin of tea. An unmistakable "brown bag lunch" stood beside them. Evidently the char brought with her the equivalent of a midnight supper. And kept other comforts there, too: shabby shoes, a beat-up pair of slippers, a pink sweater. Several cheap cotton uniforms hung from hooks, together with a typically British lightweight raincoat.

Thank you, God, I thought fervently, lifting the raincoat down with shaking fingers. It was looser and longer and dowdier than I would have worn—not enough to make me look a caricature, just enough to change my looks entirely. Let me be right about that, dear God, let me be right, I thought, for there was no way of checking in a mirror.

I must hurry. With the door shut I could not tell whether the vacuuming was still going on. Feverishly, I slipped on the shoes. They did not fit. I would have to risk the ones I'd been wearing not being recognized. I took them from my purse and thrust my bruised feet into them. The purse would have to be left; it was far too distinctive. What did I need? Wallet, Ellen's passport, Dad's picture. My room key.

Where to put the wallet? There was no way to be sure it would not fall out of my bra. I thought furiously and then, meticulously, took my shoes off and put my pantyhose back on. I thrust the wallet down their front. Try falling out of there, I thought, wanting crazily to giggle. Fortunately, the coat was shapeless enough to conceal the bulge. By a miracle, there was a headscarf in the pocket of the raincoat. Swiftly, I bundled my hair back under it, and tied it beneath my chin. Then, with trembling fingers, I snapped the eye makeup case open and peered at myself in its tiny mirror.

It would work. Pray God and not too much moonlight, it would work. Struck by a thought, I took the makeup and added heavy black lines above and below my eyes. The transformation was complete. I no longer looked like Ellen Robards, and I certainly didn't look like me. I looked, in fact, remarkably like a lot of the working girls I'd seen on Oxford Street. And older; definitely older.

The makeup, my room key and Ellen's passport I thrust into the raincoat pocket and jammed the purse down behind the tall cans of floor cleanser. With luck, I would be able to retrieve it later.

With luck.

I pulled the headscarf further forward to shadow my eyes, took a deep breath and yanked out the light. Then, my heart hammering, I opened the closet door.

The vacuum was still humming, closer now. Swiftly, stealthily as a cat, I slunk down the hall, keeping against the wall, well away from the upstairs light. Slipped the bolt on the front door. Would it open easily? It did. With a roaring in my ears and a sharp glance toward the still-empty stairwell, I forced myself to breathe slowly, in and out. Then, as calmly as I would have tried to look at the commencement of a gymnastics competition, I opened the door wide enough to pass through and stepped outside. Casually, the way a girl would do going home from work. Shut the door behind me in the same way, careful not to look back at it, doing so as if I'd done it a hundred times. Went down the steps matter-of-factly: a London char anxious to catch a bus but not otherwise in a rush.

Remember to walk purposefully, not looking around. Remember to walk differently—walks and posture angles could be recognized. Don't glance at windows; don't flick a look at side streets. Don't try to find the watchers. Just keep moving. And for the love of God act as if you know where you're going!

I was around the square. Turn this corner, and I was out of Covington Close. Was someone hiding behind those trash cans? No. And the shadow moving in the alley was a cat's.

I was down one block . . .two . . . and not a thing had happened. With infinite relief I saw bright lights ahead of me. A main thoroughfare, a late-hours pub, and, blessedly, a bus stop. I was too afraid to risk the enclosed darkness of the Underground.

Two elderly women were waiting for a bus, and some punk rockers spilled out of the pub. Their eyes traveled over me without curiosity and moved on. The bus bore down on us; thank God, a bus heading toward Victoria Station. If I had to sit up all night, that of all others would be the place to do it. That, or the fountain in Piccadilly Circus—it was always crawling with hosteling students and their knapsacks. If someone was going to try to kill me, he surely wouldn't do so beneath Piccadilly's all-night lights.

It was the first time I'd allowed myself to form that thought in words.

I climbed onto the bus after the two women. Looked quickly at the chart to learn the fare. Money—all my money was in my wallet, not reachable. *Fool*, I thought bitterly, and scrabbled in the raincoat pocket.

There were two twenty-pence pieces. Just what I needed. If Dad wrote this up in a book, his editor would tell him he was overworking coincidence. And Dad would grin and say the ways of Providence don't always follow the laws of probability. My eyes stung, and something choked my throat.

The conductor was in front of me, a young West Indian. "Where to, luv?" Hand him the two coins. Take the ticket. Nod when he says I'm working late tonight, aren't I, ducks. Pull into myself in the seat and wonder whether anyone is staring. At last, blessedly, the lights of Victoria. Stores, theaters, pubs, and around the next corner or so would be the station. A light rain had started falling. Through the spattered windows, the neon signboards shimmered—movie billboard, pub sign, streetlights, cross.

There was a church, a big brown bulk of a church, and it had a sign on it. *Youth Shelter.*

I tugged on the bell cord, and when the bus glided to a stop, I got off.

15

The sun was cool and pale and bright, and the air was fresh. It was five minutes to ten the next morning, and I was standing breathless before the high, gilt-touched wrought-iron gates of the Royal Botanical Gardens at Kew.

Those gates would not swing open until ten. Five more minutes to wait. I wondered, feverishly, if I were in time, if Dad had been forced yet to reveal my escape. What would happen to him? How long could he keep Mr. Piggott from guessing where I'd come . . . and how I'd known to come here?

I could not afford to even think about that. Those apprehensions had haunted me all through the hours since I'd left the house in Covington Close. When I'd gotten off that bus in Victoria, I'd gone straight to the church youth shelter, wiping off some of the heavy eye makeup before I entered. If I looked strange, no one said so. The young clergyman who welcomed me probably thought I was a runaway or a prostitute, but he asked no questions. He gave me tea and biscuits, offered me supper, which I declined, showed me into a dormitory room filled with metal two-decker beds. There were a few other girls there, but they too asked nothing, volunteered nothing either. I chose a bottom bunk and lay in it on my back, poring over the Kew Gardens map, trying to commit it to my memory.

In the morning I'd risen early, only to learn from the young minister that the gardens did not open to the public until ten a.m. Would Dad be able to stall Piggott and company that long? At least it meant I could take the slow-traveling bus, rather than risk traveling on the Underground.

Once again I *looked* different. The girl in the next bunk had said, "Lovely outfit, ducks," when she saw me studying my prairie skirt and shirt, wondering if they'd be too obvious, even under the too-large coat, if I wore them in the daytime. So I'd swapped with her for a pair of jeans and a checked shirt. I was beginning to feel like an actress. Except, for actresses, stage-fright was not literally a matter of life and death.

So here I was, and all I had to do was be calm and keep my wits about me. Actually, surprisingly, I had gotten some sleep last night, but not near enough. My hands felt in the jeans pockets for the tablespoon and knife that I'd concealed there. I'd stolen them, without a qualm, from the shelter kitchen.

The gates were opening. A man in a uniform was coming forward. There was another, younger man nearby in the uniform and helmet of the British bobby. Would I be able to get to him if I needed police assistance? *Ought* I turn to him? Or would that make things worse? *Calm down*, I told myself fiercely. I bought my ticket and went past the guard, not looking at him.

I was inside the walls of Kew, and everything that was England in the spring was spread out before me. Coolness and sweetness and bird calls and a bewilderment of greens. Someday I want to come here when I can really see it, I thought dazedly, making plans for the future as if they were a lifeline.

I was past the orientation house with its gleaming white walls and Palladian windows. The Broad Walk, tree-lined, led straight before me to the pond. I could go halfway down this open expanse and then cut right toward the rhododendron dell, or I could bear right here, down a narrower side path much more secluded—also faster.

Deliberately, I turned right. And as I got further from the entry buildings, I went faster and faster. There was hardly anyone there so early in the day: two young women pushing strollers toward the duck pond; a couple of workmen over by the water-lily house. Otherwise—no one. The lilac grove engulfed me, and the air was heady with their fragrance.

Poplar trees, swaying in the breeze; magnificent cedars; tiny violet flowers among the ground cover; slatted wooden benches; and wandering paths of pale gray cement. I could, so easily, have just drowned in the evidence of my senses. But the tension that never left me warned me I must use those senses as armor and antenna. Even the twittering of the birds sounded unnatural to my ears. The trees loomed higher, shutting out the light. I was almost running now.

Suddenly, in the midst of the trees, the path divided. The way off to the left went back toward spreading lawns and sunlight; the two forks leading forward twisted out of sight into dark shapes against the sky. The right path led uphill; the left one down. That faint mark on the map lay between the two; the rhododendron groves were there. Beyond the right-hand path, just beyond it, lay the walls of Kew, and beyond that the river. I turned right.

I went up into darkness, up and then down again along a path that disappeared from view behind the great bushes with their shiny black-green leaves. Sunlight arrowed among them, falling on pine needles and underbrush. The air smelled moist. I was completely enclosed, and the skin on my neck began to prickle.

I stopped, and there was not a sound. I moved again, and then I heard it, a faint rustling. My eyes saw nothing. A branch cracked, and I was paralyzed.

My mind was not. My mind clicked like a computer, willing my breathing into a regular pattern, willing my legs to move, fighting back the panic inch by inch. Hide? Run? Move like a cat and make no sound? I chose the latter. I told myself rationally that there was no sound reason to be afraid, but my rational mind knew better.

I moved two steps, and it came again, that faint rustling. I stopped, swivelled round, peering into the dimness of the undergrowth. Dad had told me once that in old English gardens there often were secret corridors deep inside hedges, that in the old days messengers or lovers or those with darker purposes had been able to slip about in them undetected. Dad: was he still bluffing through that deadly game of poker?

Silence, except for bird song far away. I took two more steps and again the rustling. I almost called out boldly, "Who's there?" Almost wanted it all to end—whatever way. But such foolhardy bravado was only for TV shows. Then another branch snapped, and I felt suddenly claustrophobic, as though a gag had been slapped over me, cutting off my breath. Involuntarily, I started to run.

I ran down the path, around the bend . . . and braked to a stop. Because, blessedly, someone was there. Not Piggott, or whoever I had feared. A workman, a perfectly ordinary workman, intently shoveling topsoil from a barrow.

"Excuse me—" He paid no attention. The crackling behind me suddenly was closer. Heedless of consequence, I ran forward, catching the man's arm. "Help me, please. I think someone's following me—"

The man shook me off. Not even looking at me, he shook his head rapidly and rotated one index finger against it. And went on shoveling. I reeled backwards, scarcely able to breathe.

A deaf mute. That was what he had been telling me, pointing to his ear. He didn't know what I was saying. He wasn't going to find out. He wasn't going to hear, if anything happened to me. I tottered backwards, swallowed hard, willed myself calm. *It was up to me. Dad thought that I could handle it.* My hand groped in my pocket, closed tight around the knife. I went by the workman swiftly, blindly, around the next turn, another. Heard the underbrush rustle. At last, when I could stand no more, I swung round and waited, breathing hard.

Something flashed in the underbrush, low to the ground. Something bright and moving. Coming towards me—

It stepped out of the shrubbery, and I almost fainted.

What was it, a parrot? It could have been, except for those two long tail feathers like a pheasant. Whatever, he was bright orange-gold, with a red face and blue head. And friendly overtures on his mind. There was no doubt whatever about that; he sauntered toward me, head on one side, looking for all the world as though he expected me to serve him breakfast. I laughed aloud, in delight and sheer relief.

"You beautiful thing . . . I'm sorry I have nothing with me." Too late, I realized I should not speak aloud. It probably doesn't matter, I thought giddily; *this* is what's been following me; there's no way anyone else could have traced me here. And the spot marked X cannot be far away. I went on, much more relaxed, and my multi-colored friend went with me.

I felt so much better I even risked taking out the marked map. Yes, this must be the place, for there were oak trees beyond the rhododendrons to the right, and far off to the left I could glimpse towering bamboo. But where? As though to lead me, the bird strode into a narrow aisle between the bushes, and I followed.

I found myself in a small open clearing rimmed by the giant rhododendrons that had concealed it. Sunlight streamed in, gilding the great fallen tree stump in the center. A tree trunk centuries old, but rotten, hollow—

Hollow.

All at once, quite clearly and acutely, I could hear every sound around me in the forest. The hum of bees, the twittering of the birds, even the slithering of a little snake that slid quite harmlessly before my feet. With a curious feeling of slow motion, of predestination, I went toward the tree trunk and knelt down, took out knife and spoon and began prying at the mass of dead leaves that filled it. The bird stayed with me, pouncing delightedly on insects I dislodged.

I took out one great scoop of leaves, another, then something near to loam. My probing fingers encountered something hard.

Carefully, carefully, I brushed the loam away, scooped more from around the edge of the square with shaking fingers. It was a wooden crate, small, tight-wedged, its top nailed down. I scrabbled at it, unable to dislodge it. Pried at the top with knife and spoon and fingers, my ears ringing.

At last, the top began to give.

It gave, and I got my fingers under it and pulled and pulled. Pulled until it came free along one side, catapulting me backwards onto the soft pine needles. The bird made an indignant comment. I pulled myself up and crept forward on my knees, sliding slightly. Reached inside, around the splintery lid.

Toys.

Small, cheap, plastic children's toys. The kind of thing you'd buy or win in an amusement arcade. I sat back on my heels, gazing at them blankly.

Behind me, a voice said quietly, "Put them down."

I did not move.

I did not have to. He came round toward me so he could face me, and there was a gun in his hand, and his gold tooth glinted. He said softly, in perfect Oxford English, "I don't want you to get hurt. Put them down, very carefully."

Not far away another voice, *not* Oxonian, said, "A very good idea, that." And chuckled.

I knew from the chuckle, even before I turned my head and stepped into the clearing, that an all-too-familiar pistol was cocked straight at me. "So we're all chums together, are we?" Piggott inquired pleasantly, jerking his head toward Esteban. "And I'm the one's bonkers, am I, thinking something's not quite straight? I don't know about your operation, but in my works we've got strong feelings about double-crosses."

Esteban was breathing hard. "Piggott," he said dangerously, "you're going over the edge, and Mr. Maguire won't like it. He told you I'd handle this, and I'm doing so, am I not?"

"No, you bloody foreigner, you're not." Piggott's voice was almost silky. My mind had detached itself again and was thinking, fantastically, that he ought to be stroking a Dickensian watchchain. "And in case you're stupid enough to think of trying any Special Forces business, I might mention that I've brought a pal along. Take the nice gun away from the little man, will you, Cliff?"

Another man, also armed, had stepped up directly behind Esteban and was sliding the weapon out of his unresisting fingers. Patting him down swiftly and professionally. Gold-tooth stood motionless, his eyes burning at me. And I—I stood like a statue, clutching my armful of cheap plastic toys.

"Very nice," Piggott said approvingly. "Now, Miss Robards, or whoever you really are, put the playthings down on the ground like the man told you, nice and easy."

Esteban said softly, looking straight at me, "Do it, Sarah."

Sarah.

Crazily, that stupid bird was still walking around watching it all like a show put on for his amusement.

Beyond us all, back toward the path, something crackled. Esteban heard it; I saw his eyes become alert. The others didn't. They didn't see his eyes.

Slowly, slowly, I eased myself down on my knees. Laid down my burden. Rose again, and I had a toy and the knife in my right hand, a toy and the spoon clutched in my left. Back in the rhododendron dell, behind the others, a shadow moved; loomed closer. Irrationally, I thought I knew to whom that shape belonged, and I could not let one of these guns be swung around toward it. Even if it were not—

It was time for Gabriel's girl to seize the balance of power, before anyone guessed what I was up to.

Rapidly, I swept my right hand up to my heart, my left hand to my head. The sun must have glittered on the plastic toys, for someone made a sharp ejaculation, swiftly suppressed. Everyone grew tense. Everyone but me.

"You'd better be careful with that gun, Mr. Piggott," I said sweetly, "if these things are what I think they are. And I guess they are, from the way you're all reacting. I've done a lot of reading the past few days about bombs. That's what these are, aren't they, plastic bombs? I don't know if these go off by friction or by a timer, but I'm pretty sure they'd explode if they got hit by bullets. So maybe you'd better not try to hit any of my vital spots, Mr. Piggott. You could get blown up, too."

The shape in the shrubbery went motionless, then crept, catlike, forward.

"Sarah," the Spaniard said softly, "you don't understand."

"Yes, I do," I said clearly. "So do our friends, here.

Don't you, Mr. Piggott?"

His face turned purple, and he moved forward a step. I clutched the toys tighter. He froze.

"I'm right, aren't I?" I said, very casually. "These things aren't predictable. They could go off at any time. From pressure . . . or being thrown . . . or if I fell on them."

The watcher stepped into the clearing and stood, braced and ready, scarcely breathing. Nobody noticed. We all just stood there. It was so crazy, it was like some bad movie. Except that you could almost hear the pounding of our hearts.

"Fergawdsakes," Piggot's sidekick muttered, licking his lips. "This crazy bird could kill us all, and she don't even care."

"You're right," I said deliberately. "I guess I'm more my father's daughter than I thought. I'd rather get wasted stopping you than wasted *by* you." I tightened my grip on the toy in my right hand, and over the perceptible hiss that greeted this said steadily, "Quent, will you please relieve these gentlemen of their weapons? Keep one yourself, and give the others to Mr. Esteban. I don't know who he is, but I gather he's a friend of Dad's."

16

"If you'd only told me what you were doing," I said somberly. "If I'd just known that you'd gone undercover . . ."

I couldn't finish. Dad looked across the table at me gravely.

"It wasn't your discretion I didn't trust, it was your safety. I didn't expect that would be jeopardized simply because I'm Gabriel Langham and you're my daughter. But if you'd known too much . . ."

Our eyes met, and all the things he hadn't said, would never say, hung in the air. If only I hadn't jeopardized his mission, and his safety, by going after him. If only I had realized, much earlier, that Langham intuition and impetuosity could be a two-edged sword—that it could be used against its user if it were not accompanied by coolheadedness, common sense, logic and caution.

It was evening, and we were in the restaurant of the Savoy. Kew Gardens and the arms merchants' arrest and my being acclaimed a heroine were hours behind us, in another life. So very much had happened in between.

As Quent had taken the guns from Cliff and Piggott, a lot of official Britishers had materialized, out of uniform but definitely armed. It still wasn't clear whether they were Special Forces, MI, CID or what. They had hand-cuffed Piggott and his goon and had only been dissuaded from handcuffing Esteban by a lot of fast talking from him and Quent. Esteban was a captain in the Spanish equivalent of Military Intelligence, it seemed, though how Quent got that piece of information I then had no idea.

All this while I was clutching those infernal plastic toys and crying out wildly that Dad must be rescued. Bomb Squad men in space suits were yelling at me not to drop those toys or move a muscle. And Quent, pale and hoarse, was shouting at me not to worry. Very, very care-fully, the bomb men approached me and pried the plastic from my frozen fingers. Then I was free to collapse into Quent's waiting arms.

Quent held me tight and stroked my hair. "It's all right, everything's all right. Your father's safe. Scotland Yard landed their hostage squad on the roof at Covington Close during the night. They couldn't move in till there was light enough to see, and of course they knew you were both in jeopardy. Especially once I told them you must be in there, too."

"How did you—"

"*I* spent yesterday going at things the other way round," Quent said grimly. "We weren't getting anywhere searching for your father. So I decided to take advantage of the fact that I had an Oxford student ID. I started do-ing 'research for a modern history paper' on London-based terrorists and their contacts. I talked to one of my professors who lives in London and to somebody at the London School of Economics who's making a study of how terrorist groups finance their operations and to the two reporters who wrote that book you bought."

He broke off. "Do you suppose your dad would give them an interview by way of thanks? Apparently they're *the* local experts. They told me Libya's been giving aid and comfort to a lot of assorted goon squads. And they gave me a description of the guy they were ninety-nine percent certain was Libya's London middleman. It matched exactly with your description of the cretin who sat by you in that pub."

"Piggott," I said automatically.

"I could think of a few other things to call him." Quint drew a deep breath. "That was when I started getting very, very scared. And when I got back to Carr-Saunders and found you'd vanished—" He couldn't go on, but his arms tightened around me in a very satisfying way.

"You still haven't explained how you found me," I said at last. "And how did Scotland Yard finally get in on the act?"

"I was out of my mind at that point," Quent said flatly. "Someone at the dorm desk finally remembered taking a message for you to meet someone somewhere, but that was all. After the experiences we'd had trying to get help from the authorities up till then, I didn't think I could go that route. Then it occurred to me that there was one person who *would* believe me, and who *could* cut through red tape. My dad. So I grabbed a cab to the Canadian Embassy, bulldozed the use of a phone there, and called him in Ottawa."

After that, things must have happened fast. Mr. Robards had made Scotland Yard, CID and the U.S.

Embassy take things very seriously. Also the Canadian embassy. Quent's life, too, had been endangered by that falling brick, he'd pointed out.

On the strength of the few things Quent could remember, he had located Uncle Tom in Madrid. I was right, Dad hadn't embarked on something this foolhardy without telling somebody what he was up to. And Tom McLean, after pointing out what a damn fool Dad was, had allowed himself to be sworn to secrecy. He had also, I suspected, provided Dad with unspecified assistance, such as passports, but that was something I'd probably never know.

If Uncle Tom had only told me! But I suspect he'd been sure my involvement would only make things worse. And how right he was.

Quent saw my face and went on quickly. "Once my father told your godfather the whole story, he was terrific. He's the one who told your embassy here that Gabe was working with someone from the Spanish Intelligence. Within five minutes, all the agencies were liasing together. It seems Interpol's been very much interested in Libya's 'London connection' for some time."

I wondered if my father had known about that. It seemed a safe bet that he had.

"I spent most of last night in an office at Scotland Yard," Quint continued, "having my brains picked and worrying about you. They got onto Covington Close, found out a Walter Maguire had rented it recently and were sure you were being held there. The name 'Maguire' made them think the Provisional IRA might be involved. I wonder if that's why your father chose it."

"I don't know yet, but I'm sure you're right. Quent, where *is* he?"

"In a police car, out by the main entrance, with strict orders to stay there." Quent laughed shakily. "I had the same orders, but the thought of sitting helplessly, knowing what you were doing— Your father told us that, as soon as we got him out. He was frantic, because the cretin had already discovered your dramatic escape and gone tearing off to get the bombs before you. Accompanied by Esteban, still playing his terrorist role, and leaving a flunky to keep your father covered. The police on the roof, of course, saw them go and had them followed. Your father's pretty wrung out, and he's got two detectives in the car with him, pumping him. Nobody was keeping that much watch on me, so I—" Quint reddened. "I just came over the wall. Me Tarzan, too, just like you last night. The police had the whole of Kew Gardens cordoned off, of course, but they couldn't empty the people out without raising an alarm. So I just blended in and did my North Woods Boy Scout bit. Then, when I got close to that clearing and saw *you*—"

Quent's face was white. "You could have got killed," he said, hard and angry. "My God, didn't you know that? You could have been killed!"

I'd known. Just as I'd known, out on that ledge. I hadn't let it sink in either time; I hadn't dared. What *had* sunk in was my responsibility for precipitating the situation. And a deep conviction that whatever danger I encountered was not heroism but simple duty.

"Come on," Quent said gently, "let's go find your father."

That had been hours ago. Since then, there had been a reunion with my father, saying little because there was so much to say. There had been an afternoon of interrogation by heaven knows how many branches of how many national authorities. I had behaved like a proper Langham, but brushed my hair back and held my head up and answered questions. But inwardly I had gotten quieter and quieter. And the ache of responsibility, an ache that even the support of Dad and Quent had not allayed, had grown. Fortunately, the whole affair was being kept as quiet as possible, in the hope that others of the network too could be trapped. So there were no TV or newspaper reporters to be faced. I don't know if I could have stood that.

Sometime during that morning, Uncle Tom had flown to London, and he was with us in the restaurant now, along with a dashingly uniformed Captain Esteban.

Uncle Tom, quite bluntly, was giving me hell. "You could have been killed. You could have gotten others killed: innocent bystanders, Sarah, and the police officers trying to rescue you. You could have jeopardized the whole case Interpol's been building up. Not to mention entering and leaving countries with a borrowed passport —a borrowed *diplomatic* passport," he emphasized, glaring at me.

"I think Sarah already knows that well enough," Dad intervened. "Besides, whatever harm she did, she more than made up for last night and today. That particular 'merchants of terror' network has probably been broken up. Thanks to that marked money, which got out and was transferred yesterday—yes, Tom, I know that was risky; that's why I didn't tell you about it. And from contacts we made, slipped remarks, we have positive proof that money donated by American citizens for civilian relief is being diverted into war materiel. That's why I had to infiltrate, get right in, to find out. And the composition of the plastic bombs proves a link with several terrorist groups and Libya. Sarah really deserves credit for saving them. Before she turned up at the house in Covington Close, I was already pretty sure the dealers weren't going to let me take delivery. And not just because she'd been on my trail. They were beginning to suspect my act."

Dad turned to me. "Didn't you say something about being followed in Spain by someone besides Esteban?"

I nodded, supplying a description of the man who'd driven me to refuge in the cathedral.

"I'd give you even money he was following me, too, when I was there. *Somebody* was."

"It was the same one," Esteban said succinctly. "We pulled him in. And they were wary of this rich Irish-American looking to buy bombs, just as we feared. You might not have managed any more than you did in Spain."

"So it was just as well," Dad went on, "that I got a message when I did from my fruit-&-veg. friend." *That* was who had phoned Dad at home, the night before he left: the Market man, and Captain Esteban. Both picking up threads Dad had started spinning last October. Both telling him the time was ripe. The fruit & veg. man had told Dad about Piggott (no wonder he was scared, I thought numbly), and Captain Esteban had engineered Dad's meeting with the ring's Torremolinos contact. The object was to see how close-knit the operation was, between countries. A lot of contraband came into the Costa del Sol from Africa. And a lot was coming into or through England. Dad was in a position to evaluate both. So after a few days in Torremolinos, "Walter Maguire," alias "Walter Brown," had been called away from La Colomba with no time to call me as he'd promised.

"Ah, yes, La Colomba." Dad grinned reminiscently. "Do you know, I don't think those fellows like me much? Especially when people started coming around asking questions."

Captain Esteban chuckled. "Not surprising. They've had experience before with questions being asked about people who've disappeared. Most recently some young girls who were lured there under false pretenses by some of our local entrepreneurs. My government takes a dim view of things like that."

"So they were giving me the runaround just to stay uninvolved with the police?"

"Apparently. And of course they didn't know a Gabe Langham had occupied Room 1327. Only a Walter Brown, who left in less than a week."

"And left his suitcase."

"I couldn't risk anyone finding out who I really was. If I got into the network as deeply as I hoped to—as I did—any whiff of my being Gabe Langham could have meant curtains."

Piece by piece, the story emerged. Why Dad had gone to Spain: Someone he'd met in Europe had given him some information on the "Libyan connection"; then only recently he'd gotten further evidence that money raised in the U.S. for relief of children orphaned by the troubles in Northern Ireland was being diverted from its

donors' purpose. And finally a month ago Captain Esteban (previous connection with Dad unspecified) had let
Dad know the Spanish authorities had gotten wind that
the Basque Separatist group was buying explosives from
dealers who were "in a regular business buying and selling for all the known terrorist organizations." So Dad had
come to Spain as "Mr. Walter Brown" (credentials sup-
plied by an unidentified source) with half a million dollars of U.S. currency (ditto).

Why Dad had gone to England: "Close to Ireland,"
Dad said succinctly. "And probably safer for the dealers
than either Italy or Germany these days. Both Bader-
Meinhoff and Red Brigade fanatics have been known to
bite the hand that feeds them." So Dad had gone there
and, following the pattern of arms dealers and terrorist
groups alike, established an "identity" and a "safe house"
. . . the house in Covington Close. Interpol and a top
secret branch of British intelligence had known about
that, though even Scotland Yard had not. They had not
dared risk bugging devices or surveillance. It had been
Dad's show until Esteban came, following me to England.

Why was Esteban following me in the first place:
Because he had had La Colomba, and Dad's luggage
there, under surveillance. He wanted to see if anyone was
investigating "Mr. Brown," if that identity or Dad's au-
thenticity as a purchasing agent was in question. "So
when a young lady shows up"—Captain Esteban bowed
gracefully in my direction—"showing a photograph, asking questions about Gabriel Langham . . . I wonder."

He had contacted Dad and provided a description.
"Then," Dad said in understatement, "I was frantic." It
was *Dad* who had written that note on Savoy stationery,

forwarding it to Esteban by some unspecified but swift means. They had hoped to force me home, without saying anything that could draw dangerous attention to me if the note were read. Only they had run into "Langham stubbornness, and Langham suspicion," Dad summed up, an equivocal expression on his face. So they had done the only things they could think of to protect me. Esteban had had me shadowed, by himself and others; he had tried to scare me into leaving; he had finally had my passport stolen. Dad had told him that that would drive me to Uncle Tom, and Uncle Tom could be counted on to take me in hand. Only I hadn't let him.

Why hadn't Uncle Tom leveled with me? "Your father would have killed me," he said flatly. "Besides, I really didn't know that much, and anything you found out, I knew, could put you both in danger." Dad, it seemed, had told Uncle Tom only enough so *someone* would know to look for him if he vanished for too long. "I told your father not to be a damn fool," Uncle Tom said flatly. "I also told him it was time he grew up and became a law-abiding citizen. No, I did not report what he was up to to the London embassy or Scotland Yard. For one thing, there wasn't any reason to then. If we government employees went around informing one another about every tidbit of gossip that comes our way, we'd never get our own work done. Every government's a bureaucracy, and the right hand never knows what the left hand's doing—any more than the Torremolinos police knew what Esteban, here, was up to with your father. Anyway, I already knew that Esteban's superiors—and I suspect, some of my own—already knew what your macho old man was up to."

When I disappeared that day in Madrid, Uncle Tom, too, was frantic. He'd gotten in touch with Esteban, and Esteban, on a hunch, had gone to London, surfacing there as Carlos.

"And it was not, repeat *not*, Sarah's presence in London alone that blew my cover," Dad said emphatically, repeating what he'd said earlier. The arms merchants and their customers, the terrorist network, have an intelligence service as complete as any a government might have. Witness the fact that they'd had Walter Brown shadowed from the first day he'd sent feelers out in Torremolinos. And the way they had picked up on me so quickly. It was ironic that they'd spotted me in London by following Carlos, who was there to guard and follow me. And Carlos had located me by remembering I'd been seen with a tall blond young man. He had identified Quentin Robards quickly, and when I'd vanished, had looked for *him*, only to learn he'd gone to London with a "sister."

No, my searching for Dad in London hadn't blown his cover, at least not so far as Gabriel Langham was concerned. But it had added to the supplier's suspicions and caused confusion. Was I a spy for the authorities or a part of Maguire's own operation or just a weirdo? That was what had bothered Piggott. And Piggott, acting like me on hunch and emotion, had first tried to get rid of me and then reeled me in. I decided he hadn't actually wanted to kill me, just get me out of the way. But after two failures, he didn't dare try again, for fear I was a spy for the authorities and someone would catch him or his cohorts.

"When Piggott showed up at Covington Close with

you," Dad said heavily, "I had no choice. I *had* to play it the way I did—gamble on your having the brains and the coolheadedness to take my cues. And by God, you did!"

"Was it worth it?" Quent asked tightly. We all stared at him, and he went on, very quietly. "You had suspicions, that's all, with no real proof. You set this whole thing up, deliberately, on the slim chance you might get that proof. You didn't have to, Mr. Langham. You're not in government service any more—as far as I know," he amended deliberately.

Dad didn't answer.

Quent went on steadily. "Even if you were in Intelligence, or whatever your government calls it, you could have been killed. *Sarah* could have been killed. She was almost killed. Was it worth it?"

"There are two ways I can answer that," Dad said at last. "As a father, and—no, come to think of it, there's only one way. I've seen too much of terrorism, kicking around the world all these years the way I have. I've seen things that never make television because they're too grisly—children killed, mutilated, blown to bits. I've seen whole generations grow from infancy to adulthood never knowing anything but war and hate. And it's always for a good cause. And there are always those, like these scum today, who are willing to capitalize on that hate and passion for their own greed. I didn't know Sarah would come after me. Perhaps I should have. I'm so used to taking care of a little girl I forget she's a young woman now, with a mind and passions of her own. But even so—I can't speak for Sarah, but for myself, yes, it was worth it. A thousand times worth it."

I said, looking straight at my father, "It was worth it for me, too. Though I only wish I'd grown up with some of your caution and ability to think clearly under pressure. I'd give anything to undo the damage I did by rushing in blindly."

"You already have," Dad said gently. "And after today I don't think anyone will question your ability to think under pressure. I know I won't."

There was silence. Then Quent said, his voice shaking slightly, "It's not my place to say it. I haven't known any of you very long. I know you—professionals —can take a lot of covert activities and danger in your stride . . ."

It occurred to me suddenly that Dad never had denied Quent's implication that he might be involved in CIA activities. And it also occurred to me that I'd probably never know the truth about that—and I didn't want to.

"—but I want to say that what I saw Sarah do in Kew Gardens today was the coolest act of bravery I expect to see in my whole life. *I* didn't trust myself, but she never faltered. For the rest of my life, I'm never going to forget—that."

Quent said, "that," but his eyes said a whole lot more. He lifted his glass of wine to me and drank, never taking those eyes off me. For the rest of my life, I thought, *I'm* going to remember this moment, now. And I knew that all those thoughts I'd been having, about the difference in our ages and the distances between New Jersey and Spain and Oxford and Ottawa, had been just needless worry.

Dad knew exactly what I was thinking—and what

I was feeling. It was that "Langham communication" again. When he spoke it was with a mixture of pride and sadness, but his tone was whimsical. "So 'Gabe's girl' really is a chip off the old block, just like Tom predicted. I suppose there'll be no keeping you out of my research after this. In fact, you're so much a part of this particular story I'll probably have to give you credit. 'By Gabriel Langham, assisted by Sarah Gabriel Langham.' How does that strike you, Sarah?"

With Quent's eyes on me, Quent's mouth curving in a slow smile as he looked at me, my spirits were fizzing like champagne.

"Don't be too sure," I said. "I may just write a book about this myself!"

And so I did.